P9-CEM-106

The Isabel Factor

The Isabel Factor

Gayle Friesen

COCHRAN PUBLIC LIBRARY
174 BURKE STREET
STOCKBRIDGE, GA 30281

KCP FICTION
An Imprint of Kids Can Press

HENRY COUNTY LIBRARY SYSTEM
HAMPTON, LOCUST GROVE, McDONOUGH, STOCKBRIDGE

KCP Fiction is an imprint of Kids Can Press

Text © 2005 Gayle Friesen

All rights reserved. No part of this publication may be reproduced, stored in a retrieval system or transmitted, in any form or by any means, without the prior written permission of Kids Can Press Ltd. or, in case of photocopying or other reprographic copying, a license from The Canadian Copyright Licensing Agency (Access Copyright). For an Access Copyright license, visit www.accesscopyright.ca or call toll free to 1-800-893-5777.

This is a work of fiction and any resemblance of characters to persons living or dead is purely coincidental.

Many of the designations used by manufacturers and sellers to distinguish their products are claimed as trademarks. Where those designations appear in this book and Kids Can Press Ltd. was aware of a trademark claim, the designations have been printed in initial capital letters (e.g., Jell-O).

Kids Can Press acknowledges the financial support of the Government of Ontario, through the Ontario Media Development Corporation's Ontario Book Initiative; the Ontario Arts Council; the Canada Council for the Arts; and the Government of Canada, through the BPIDP, for our publishing activity.

Published in Canada by
Kids Can Press Ltd.
29 Birch Avenue
Toronto, ON M4V 1E2

Published in the U.S. by
Kids Can Press Ltd.
2250 Military Road
Tonawanda, NY 14150

www.kidscanpress.com

Edited by Charis Wahl
Designed by Marie Bartholomew
Interior graphics by Sherill Chapman
Printed and bound in Canada

CM 05 0 9 8 7 6 5 4 3 2
CM PA 05 0 9 8 7 6 5 4 3 2 1

Library and Archives Canada Cataloguing in Publication

Friesen, Gayle
    The Isabel factor/ by Gayle Friesen.

ISBN 1-55337-737-0 (bound).   ISBN 1-55337-738-9 (pbk.)

I. Title.

PS8561.R4956I83 2005   jC813'.54
C2004-906029-5

Kids Can Press is a *l'©rUs*™ Entertainment company

For my crazy sisters: Barb, Patti and Bren.
Swaf fwas.

ACKNOWLEDGMENTS

Thanks again go to the intrepid Charis, the attentive Jennifer, and to Fred for his well-timed encouragement. Also thanks to Alison and Christy, the best re-readers ever. Thanks always to my family.

Chapter One
Ship Sets Sail

The ferry horn bellows three deafening, unexpected blasts. This shouldn't come as a big surprise — it's what ferry horns do — but because I'm in a daze, the noise makes me tumble off the bulkhead, which in turn causes the letter that I'm about to rip open (even though I promised to wait until I saw the first tip of Kairos Island) to fall from my lap where a gust of wind plucks it up and sends it pirouetting across the deck where it skids to a stop just under the railing, poised to plummet into the pale pink Pacific. Yeah, I know, that's a really long sentence with a lot of p's, and the ocean isn't really pink. My English teacher (and sponsor of the school paper), Mr. Hong, says that journalists should restrict themselves to the unvarnished, unbiased truth. Say it clearly, accurately, concisely. Just the facts.

I guess this is what happens when you mess with a promise: the elements conspire against you. I shuffle over to the letter, grab it and stuff it into the pocket of my cargo pants.

"Good save."

I look around to see where this disembodied voice has come from. Not far from me slouches a girl — at least I think she's a girl. She has a cap of hair that makes her appear not entirely human, maybe even a little otherworldly. It's every color of the rainbow and a few others besides. Each tuft — feather almost — is streaked a brilliant shade of either scarlet, orange, fuchsia, emerald green or sapphire blue. She looks like she could fly away on the next gust of wind. I realize that I am staring.

"Oh, right," I mutter. I return to my little corner where I huddle in for the rest of the trip.

This is exactly the beginning I would expect to this summer. It was supposed to be the summer of a lifetime, but the elements have conspired and that's hardly ever a good thing.

Chapter Two
Girl Takes Tumble

Every story has a beginning, a middle and an end. I need to begin at the beginning.

It was a normal June day. School had ended the week before, and I was getting ready to go to camp with Zoe, like we'd done for the last seven years. We were going to be CITs: Counselors In Training. Some people called CITs glorified slaves (lots of kitchen and latrine duties), but we knew it was going to be our best summer yet. It was also the last official summer of our childhood. Since the last of anything is always sad, we figured we deserved a brilliant send-off to the world of adulthood or, as Zoe insisted on calling it when her mom was in earshot, adultery.

Zoe and I had been friends since the first grade. We were a pair. A pair of socks, my dad would say. My dad says a lot of corny things, but I liked this one. She was the left foot; I was the right. Together we had things covered. We were the flip side of the same coin. Yin and yang. (That's Chinese for something I don't remember.) Peanut butter and jelly. You get the picture.

Zoe was daring, restless and hardly ever afraid. There was always excitement around her, even if you weren't exactly the type of person who liked to do daring things. (Me.) She wasn't afraid to live life; I wasn't afraid to take notes. Like I said ... a pair.

Zoe's mom phoned two days before we were set to leave. "Anna, dear," she sighed. (She always called me that.) "Zoe's had an accident."

"Zoe" and "accident" in the same sentence wasn't all that unusual, but I felt in my gut that there was more to it. I heard myself ask, "What do you mean?" like I was having one of those out-of-body experiences.

"She's broken her arm. In three places, of course."

I only thought about the "of course" later. Her mom was convinced that Zoe's extreme Zoe-ness could be modified if she'd only try harder, and sometimes I agreed; but I wasn't sure that a person could control how many places their arm broke. I'd need more details. Facts. Unvarnished.

"What happened?"

"She was climbing in the barn at her Auntie Zelda's farm. She said she was trying to save a kitten." (For sure there had to be more to it.) "In any event, she'll be out of commission for the summer. They're considering traction."

I had an immediate image of Zoe constrained by cords and pulleys and plaster casts with only slits where her eyes and nostrils should be.

"Oh, I knew you'd be upset, Anna. You've been

such a good friend to our Zoe." She was on the verge of tears. "Camp will be out of the question this year."

There it was. The reason for my involuntary gut clench. "No, no. She can still come. We'll figure something out." I could see a hospital bed being wheeled into the cabin, a ramp being constructed by three or four well-muscled workmen, Zoe flirting with each and every one of them as she was wheeled across the threshold, a rose, possibly, between her teeth. "When can I see her?"

"She should be ready for visitors tomorrow. Now, Anna, dear, can I speak to your mother?"

My mother oohed and aahed in all the appropriate places as Zoe's mom went over the details of the accident. "Oh, the poor thing," Mom cooed. "Oh, you poor thing," she added. I urged her to speed up the empathy with a hand motion, mouthing the words, "What's going on?" She scowled and shook her head at me, knitting her eyebrows in an effort to show me how pained she was on behalf of her friend. I slumped into a chair and tried to piece together what was happening. After my mother's third "Oh, my" and the fourth "Oh, dear," I gave up. When she finally hung up, I was ten years older, married and pregnant with her first grandchild.

"So, what did she say?"

"Well, she told you, didn't she? Zoe's had an accident. She's broken her arm in —"

"Three places. I know, I know. Is she serious about

Zoe not going to camp? She can't be serious." My mother's face didn't shift, not a muscle; it was her Rock of Gibraltar face. She folded her arms across her chest. I also crossed my arms. "Well, then, I'm not going, either. No way."

"Your concern for your friend is overwhelming, Anna," she sighed. (If my mother dropped sighing from her repertoire of responses, she would have a lot of free time on her hands.)

"I'm concerned. Of course I am. I want to see her right away. I'm just saying —"

"First things first. What are her favorite flowers? Do you think we should bake something? We should bake."

"Tulips. Brownies. I want to go now."

"Minnie said we should wait until tomorrow. Apparently she's pretty doped up. Zoe, that is. Do you need some help with the brownies?"

"No, no." Would a dessert of refined sugar and cocoa change the course of our lives? Well, would it?

My mother turned around at the door. "And don't even think about using a mix."

Apparently it would if baked from scratch. I groaned, to which she responded, "You always go for the easy way out."

I didn't think this was fair, but I knew better than to argue when my mother was talking about doing *the right thing*. And it seemed that right now *the right thing* was homemade brownies.

As I stirred the ingredients, adding the eggs carefully to avoid broken shells, which might indicate lack of concern, I regretted not going with Zoe to her aunt's farm. I had decided to stay home because I wanted to get things ready for camp, but clearly I had made the wrong choice. If I had gone with her, this wouldn't have happened. I didn't even need the details to know this for sure. I would have seen disaster looming. I am very good at spotting looming disaster.

But I wasn't there. So instead, I baked brownies.

The next morning I woke up early, excited in spite of myself. There was something thrilling about accidents, their unpredictability, maybe. Zoe lying in a hospital, helpless — reaching to push her nurse-come-help-me button, but being too weak — was weird, yet compelling. I could see myself holding her hand, telling her everything would be okay. "I'm here for you," I would say quietly, filled with confidence-inspiring strength. "I knew you'd come," she would whisper back.

Those thoughts (Mr. Hong would call them sentimental) ran through my brain as the morning dragged by and my mother insisted on a nutritious breakfast because, as everyone knows, a healthy breakfast is the cornerstone to a long and successful life, and it didn't really matter that my best friend was wasting and pining away in the dark hollow reaches of some godforsaken hospital.

Dad finally left for work. Grady, my kid brother, ambled over to his best friend's house after finishing my eggs. Mom tidied up the kitchen (the other cornerstone for a long and successful life). Finally we were ready to go.

"Do you have the brownies?" she asked.

"I have the brownies," I said calmly.

"I picked up a magazine when I went to get the flowers. Will she like *O*?"

"Um, because she has so much in common with Oprah? Did they not have *Seventeen*?" Less calm.

Mom shuddered. "That's such garbage. The entire issue was on 'How to please your man.' I mean, honestly. It's just so disempowering —"

"She'll love *O*." If I didn't agree, she'd launch into one of her speeches about when she was young and Barry Manilow sang songs that had the whole world singing and people didn't feel the need to show their belly buttons at the drop of a hat and life was *obladi, oblada*, and we'd never get to the hospital. "Very appropriate," I added.

"That's what I thought." She seemed relieved, and then she began looking for her keys until I pointed out that they were in her hand.

Appropriate is very important to my mother. It's right up there with doing the right thing, flossing and always having tampons along just in case. And now it seemed brownies and Oprah were at the front of the line.

At the hospital, we saw Zoe's mom in the parking lot. I knew that if I had to stop and make pleasant conversation with Minnie (that's her actual name), who out-moms my mother to the power of forever, I would lose any composure I still had and, possibly, my breakfast. I told my mother that I would find Zoe and meet them in the room.

"I'll just ask at the information desk," I said, sliding away even as Minnie loped up, bursting with concern and news.

I got a little nervous when I reached Zoe's room because it suddenly hit me that Zoe was inside that disinfected, sterile place. I peered around the corner, letting only my head and part of my shoulders show. She didn't have a private room.

A pale girl, about nine or so, waved to me as though I might be the entertainment minus a red nose. I put my finger across my lips and whispered, "Shh."

"Hey," she shouted. "Do you have Jell-O?"

Okay, so maybe she didn't think I was a clown. Obviously she had mistaken me for a nurse. It was an honest mistake. I was wearing a white T-shirt. I "shh'd" her again, but this had the effect of a red cape on a bull.

"Did you bring presents?" she bellowed.

I walked to the side of her bed. I could see Zoe, but it looked like she was sleeping. "I'm here to visit my friend. Do you want a brownie?"

She nodded energetically. I dug out a chunk of brownie and handed it to her. She looked so eager that I panicked. "You're not diabetic, are you?"

She shook her head. "Appendix. I'm going home today." Honestly, she sounded like a lumberjack. I handed over the brownie.

Gayle Friesen

I walked over to Zoe's bed beside the brownie-eating-appendix-missing Paul Bunyan. I pulled the curtain with a zing along the track, providing a flimsy wall between us and the rest of the world. Zoe lay there, still and motionless, although, strictly speaking, I suppose that's redundant. (Sorry Mr. Hong.) But I need both words because it is so rare to see Zoe either still or motionless. She looked sick and it unnerved me. She looked sick and injured and still. And watching her, I felt sick and injured.

"Zoe, it's me," I said. Her arm was hooked up to a contraption. My imagination in this case had not been far off. There weren't pullies, but there was a cast. The hundred times we jumped off trampolines, sundecks, picnic tables, swing sets, the wharf at camp flashed through my mind like one of those "remember when" segments at an awards show. A tear snaked down my face and ended up on the tip of my nose.

One eye popped open, wide and clear, then the other. "Hey, babe. Got you."

"Did not," I said, wiping my eyes and nose with a swipe of my shirt. "Were you awake the whole time?"

"Not my fault. If I don't pretend to sleep" — Zoe lowered her voice to a whisper — "Gabby next door talks the whole time. But then you came in and I couldn't resist."

I pulled a chair beside the bed and sat down. "How are you, anyway? I can't believe you aren't coming to camp." I hadn't meant to say this quite so soon, but

18

there it was, standing right in front of us like an elephant, too obvious to ignore.

Her eyes got all watery. I felt bad. "No, really, how are you?"

"It hurts."

"I'm sorry. I'm so sorry. Were you really trying to save a kitten?"

"I love animals." She sounded defensive. My reporter's ears burned.

"And?"

"And nothing."

"And what?"

"And, okay. Do you remember the boy who lives next to my aunt? Alan?"

"Alan the Weasel?"

Zoe nodded her head, and then shook it with equal vigor plus a Mona Lisa smile. "He is *so* not a weasel anymore."

"Aha." The plot, as they say, was thickening. If a boy was involved, it made more sense. But why Alan the Weasel, even if he was Alan the Former Weasel — which, by the way, I would have to see to believe. My investigative instincts were piqued. "How is Alan involved in your broken arm?"

"You know the beam that stretches across the barn?"

"The one that looks like the high wire at the circus?"

"Alan bet me that I couldn't walk across it in less than thirty seconds — his record."

"Say no more." The missing piece: competition — the thrill of it. Zoe said it made her eyeballs pulse. And Zoe was almost always first. It didn't matter if it was track and field, first string on the basketball team, star of the school play or captain on our swim team. Zoe's thirst for first was an unending source of amazement. She didn't always make it, but that didn't stop her from going for it. The only place I came close to her was on the swim team, but even then I only ever came second to Zoe.

Zoe has two older brothers and two younger brothers. Their family motto is *We don't do anything just for fun.* Once when we were riding our bikes to the pool, I fell off my bike into some blackberry brambles on the side of the road. Zoe didn't even notice. I arrived, scratched and bloody, about ten minutes after her. She said she hadn't heard me call out. I asked why she didn't even look, and she said, "Oh, no, you never look back." Like it was some kind of golden rule. "Were we racing?" I asked. "It's always a race," she answered, seemingly shocked that she had to explain this.

"Okay, so you were trying to beat the record," I recapped. "And that's when you fell?"

"Are you kidding? I did it in twenty-eight seconds."

"Well?" I prodded. "Then when?"

"Are you sure you want to hear all this?"

I leaned back in the green vinyl hospital chair and flipped open an imaginary pad. I wetted an imaginary pencil on my tongue and prepared myself for a long, complicated story. With Zoe, any tale usually moved in three or four directions at a time. She was the broken compass of circumstance. (Okay, that needs some work.)

"Just the facts, ma'am," I reminded her. "Name?"

She smiled prettily. "Zoe Marie Desdemona Jarvis."

I peered over the top of my imaginary pad. "Stick to the facts, ma'am."

"Zoe Marie Jarvis."

"So, could you tell me what *actually* happened on the morning of the accident, Ms. Jarvis?"

"Okay. So Alan leaves after I kick his butt on the beam walk, right? But I'm thinking, twenty-eight seconds? Phht. I can do so much better than that, and so I go back up."

"You decided to compete against yourself? Phht?"

Zoe looked a little sheepish, but only for a second. "The problem was I had to time myself, which meant looking down at my watch."

"And that's when you fell."

"No. Twenty seconds — I was almost there. Then the damned rooster crowed."

"Which is what damned roosters do."

"But not, like, in the middle of the morning."

"So that's when you fell?"

"No."

I slouched even farther down in the chair and put my watch to my ear. "What day is it? How long have I been here?"

"Okay, okay," she said. "So the damned rooster

crows and I think, that is a very cool sound, but I bet I could be more convincing."

"Oh, Zoe." I wrapped my arm around my head.

"Well, if I'm going to be an actor, I need to be able to get inside the character, right?"

I started whimpering. The picture of Zoe on a beam, out-crowing a rooster made perfect sense in Zoe-land. It was such a great country, too. But even so. "And that's when you fell."

"And that's when I fell."

I got up and hugged her.

"I didn't fall on purpose."

"I know," I said. "I knew there had to be more to it than a kitten."

"I had to tell my mother something. She'd freak out if she knew I was walking the beam on a dare."

"No kidding."

"Mothers." We said this at the same time.

It always comforted us to think that our mothers were at the bottom of things otherwise inexplicable. They didn't understand us. They wanted to, tried, and failed. Because we were something new. Maybe we didn't know exactly who or what we were, but we knew that whatever they said we were, that's exactly who and what we weren't.

"You have to go without me," Zoe said.

"I don't want to go without you. It won't be any fun."

"Sure it will. You're the fun one, remember?"

"No, I'm not. You are, remember?"

"No, remember, you are?"

We did this for quite a while. The other nice thing about best friends is that they find the same lame things funny. "I can't," I said, finally.

"You have to. BTBD." (Best Times Before Dying.)

Zoe once told me about an aunt and uncle of hers who had been married for sixty years. When her uncle died, Zoe went to the funeral. Her aunt stood by the casket, smiled deeply and passionately into the dead face of her husband and said, "We had the best time, didn't we?"

Zoe told me later that it was the most important moment of her life. She knew then what she wanted. Well, it wasn't so much that she wanted someone to look down at her dead face and say, "We had the best time, didn't we?" It was more that she wanted to really live her life.

We decided then that our whole lives would be full of Best Times Before Dying. BTBD. That's what this summer was supposed to be.

But not separately — without Zoe it didn't seem possible. We were a team, a pair. How often do you hear about yin, or yang for that matter, on its own? Never.

Chapter Three
Truth Overrated

Packing for camp was a stupid, endless chore, like a slog through mud in a rainstorm. My mother watched me nervously. "Honestly, Anna," she groaned. "Let me do it."

"I don't see why I have to go." I slumped against the wall.

"You've been looking forward to this all year," she said briskly, as if brisk might be just the thing to convince me.

"No. Zoe and I were looking forward to it."

She rifled through my top drawer and emerged with an armful of my underwear. "Mom, please." There comes a moment your life when you really don't need to see your mother and your panties in the same room together.

She handed the lump of lingerie over with a drawn-out sigh. (She wasted at least three seconds of her life on that one.) "Maybe it's really for the best."

"Mother!"

"Not the accident, of course. Just you and Zoe.

You've been acting like conjoined twins for years now, and you always keep yourself in her shadow. Maybe it's time for a little independence."

I stuffed clothes into my suitcase without even pretending to fold them. I could feel her eyes on me, but I kept my back turned as I tried to close the bulging bag.

"Let me do that," she said, pushing me aside. "I think you've brought everything you own." She pulled out the T-shirts and began to fold. "And how much lip gloss do you really need?"

I kept my mouth shut. I suspected that my mother had doctored up somebody else's childhood photos to back up her story that once upon a time she was young.

"I'm glad Zoe is your friend, Anna. I've been glad since you brought her home that first day of school. You know I love her, too. But there will be other girls there. Jennifer is going, right?"

Jennifer Clements. The kind of friend every mother wants their daughter to have. She was pretty, popular, poised, polite, occasionally persnickety but never around parents. (And political.) Sorry. Runaway alliteration again.

Zoe and I were friends with Jennifer in eighth grade before she moved to the upper echelon — upgraded, you could say. Cashed in her frequent flier points for a better seat on the airplane of life. No hard feelings (although she did tell us that we were a little immature), that's just the way high school is. You find your level — and Jennifer's level was greatness. She was going to rule the world one day, and you can't really start too soon if that's your goal.

Zoe was really ticked off about it. She huffed and puffed for a few days, muttering, "Who does she think she is?" and "Does she think she's better than us?"

I answered, "Jennifer Clements" and "Yes."

This infuriated Zoe until I reminded her that we still had each other. That was all we needed, right? So we just pulled our knot tighter and continued on our way. And it wasn't as if Jennifer stopped being our friend entirely. She still hung out with us occasionally. It was the old Solar System of Friendship situation. You have your Sun — Jennifer and her group — and then you have your orbiting planets. I'd say Zoe and I were Mars. Not bad, really. Seriously, you could be Pluto.

Mom was still folding things in neat, anal, Freudian piles and placing them in my suitcase. "But sometimes in life we just have ourselves, honey. And sometimes it has to be enough. We have to figure out that we are enough."

At that point she seemed to realize that she was recycling her life-affirming clichés, and she did the mother drift. Her eyes glazed over and she went to the Barry Manilow place. "Can you finish up here?" she asked.

"Yep."

She went to get ready for her Book Club meeting, which involved the preparation of small food and large martinis.

I unfolded each article of clothing she'd folded and crushed it into the suitcase haphazardly, where it could be free to wrinkle if that's what it wanted to do. I could almost hear Zoe laughing at me. I listened to grouchy music (punk), moved on quickly to angry music (metal), and finally tried soothing music (Sinatra). Nothing worked. Tried a *Simpsons* rerun. First time that didn't work. Finally I decided to eavesdrop on the Menopause-Preparedness Group, a.k.a. the Book Club.

The group had started with an eye toward great literature, awareness expansion and exotic teas: *One Hundred Years of Solitude*. To my knowledge, they never got past page ten. Then somebody (Maxine?) took a wrong turn at the bookstore and ended up in the self-help section. Somebody else (Janine?) discovered the liquor store and ended up in the gin section. And, voilà, the Book Club took flight — clumsily at first, like a heron. Then it soared.

Tonight's topics ranged from Maxine's Botox injections (You look rested!) and Nancy's hot flashes (Open the windows, right *&%# now!) to Janine's meddling mother (Still? How depressing!) and finally Minnie's injured daughter, Zoe.

I leaned closer, sipped my soda and listened to the details of Zoe's fall. Her aunt found her nestled in the hay like a broken bird. I hated the sound of that. I hated the murmurs of understanding that trickled across the room. And I hated the way this was becoming Minnie's story. No mention of Zoe's plans, only Minnie's pain — how difficult and willful teen-agers could be. Minnie's pain? I needed another soda.

When I returned, my mother was talking, slightly tipsy. It was time for her pain. She was worried about me going to camp alone. Could I handle the independence? Did I know how to be on my own? That got quite a few sympathetic, trickling murmurs as they agreed that it was difficult to find one's true self and wasn't life complicated? Then there was a clinking of glasses.

Well, I thought, so there, perched in the La-Z-Boy recliner, was my wonderful support system. Yep, her — the one with the half-empty martini glass, surrounded by one hundred years of unread solitude. So much for "sometimes we just have ourselves. And sometimes that has to be enough."

Mr. Hong likes to say — well, a million, trillion things. One of the things he likes to say is "bullshit." This has gotten him into quite a bit of trouble with the school board. Once, he agreed to find a substitute expression, but when kids went home quoting his "steaming pile of defecation," the board gave up. But besides "bullshit," Mr. Hong likes to say "The truth lies somewhere, if we knew but where."

Well, I knew exactly where. I was on my own. I was afraid. And I wasn't enough. Facts. And if Zoe had been there, crouched on the floor beside me, slurping a soda, the whole thing would have been hysterically funny.

One day later, I was deposited on the ferry that would transport me across the ocean to that tiny island that was to be my home for a month. Mom and Dad and Grady waved from the dock. I could hear my mother's voice as the ferry pulled away from the slip. "Just be yourself." I stopped waving.

My family gave one final, embarrassing, collective yip and then left. A knot tied itself around my guts and gave a good pull as the ferry hoisted itself away from the shore with a roar of the engines.

That's when I found a place that was protected from the wind and took out the letter Zoe gave me when we dropped by to say good-bye. She made me swear not to open it until I caught a glimpse of the island's shore, but the temptation became overwhelming. That's when the elements conspired to steal the letter and I ran into mysterious Feather-girl.

And now we're up to speed.

But a promise is a promise and I decide to walk around the deck until it is truly time to read the letter.

Chapter Four
Truth Embellished

It's a beautiful day, but the wind is sharp. I pull my jacket closely around me against the sting of the cold. I'm leaning over the railing, watching the ship churn up a furrow of grayish-white foam, when a flutter of flower petals drifts past one by one. I look around to see where they've come from. At the corner of the ferry stands the girl with the rainbow of colors in her hair, looking like an elaborate Christmas craft. I sidle along the railing in an attempt to get closer, but I also want to appear as though I am not moving toward her. I stop and give a sidelong glance to see if she's noticed. She hasn't, so I keep sidling. When I look again, she is still busy plucking petals from a daisy and tossing them into the wind. She's doing it methodically, taking her time. I watch her dismember the flower and I wonder if she's doing the old "loves me, loves me not" routine. Maybe she's left a boyfriend behind. Maybe he's French or Polynesian or British. Maybe he's Prince William. Probably not. Maybe he's a hairdresser, which would explain the hairdo. (Zoe would call it the hair-don't.) I'm thinking of all the possible boyfriends for this complete stranger and wondering if I should say hello, when a gust of wind ushers her words over to me. They are low, but I can just make them out.

"Hates me," she says. Then, "Hates me not."

I change my mind about saying hello. I definitely decide against asking about the French/Polynesian/British boyfriend who may be Prince William or a hairdresser. As I move over to the bulkhead where I've stowed my stuff, I hear her, one last time.

"Hates me." I look down and see the now-bald flower flutter past into the wake, where it is swallowed whole.

I can't stop myself from twisting my neck around. She's disappeared.

I move back to the bulkhead and pull my backpack onto my lap for a windbreak. (I'm not taking any chances. I'll definitely wait until I spot Kairos Island before I read the letter.) Rainbow-girl keeps popping into my head because, even though it's a big boat with lots of people, there is a chance she's going to my camp. There could be a story here. Everyone has a story, says Mr. Hong. You just have to find it. When I'm working on an article for the paper, I occasionally add details that, strictly speaking, aren't true, but they make the story sound much better. Apparently this is called "embellishment" and is not an acceptable journalistic technique. Less is more, says Mr. Hong.

When I look up, I realize I have missed the first

sighting of Kairos Island. I quickly pull the letter out of the torn envelope and skim past the greeting: *Hey, Babe. Can you see him? Can you?* (We always refer to the island as a him because the sea is a she and ships are shes so it just seems fair and more balanced.) *Oh, I can't believe I'm not their.* (Zoe finds spelling a waste of time.) *I want you to have a great summer, even though I won't be they're.* ("There, there," I mutter.) *I want you to have the summer we planned to have together ... I'll be with you in sprit.* (Now I'm overcome with homesickness and regret for having corrected her word usage and at the same time I'm thinking she probably means "spirit.") *Don't forget me. BTBD. Love, Zoe.* Then there is a PS, which seems kind of strange. I guess she means it as a comfort. *PS,* it reads. *You'll be fine. Everybody likes you.*

I read the short letter over and over until I've memorized it. I had hoped it would be longer, but I tell myself that less is more, although with Zoe more is usually more. Forget her? What a weird idea. Forgetting Zoe would be like forgetting to wake up early on Christmas morning or forgetting to eat or to wear underwear. Zoe was a necessity.

The loudspeaker announces that we have arrived. As the boat lumbers up to the dock, the familiar smells and sights of the island hit me as though I've never been gone: creosote from the pilings, sun-baked seaweed crusted on the edges of the shore, salt water mixed with something ... maybe day-old grease from the diner across the road. All of it reaches me at once, carrying memories of summers past. I learned how to swim here, handle a kayak, make really ugly pottery that my mom still uses. (A twinge of homesickness hits me. I bat it away.)

As I disembark, I see familiar faces. We shriek loudly. Jennifer, Benita, Charmaine. I hope they won't ask why I didn't look for them on the ferry. They don't. Quick overview: Jennifer is medium-build, very strong and never wears a shirt that doesn't show off her well-defined arms. In a word, she tends toward bossiness (as befits the Queen of the Sun). Benita is blonde this year as though she ran headlong into a bottle of bleach and the bleach won. She leans toward bored. Charmaine has a tattoo! No, wait, it's fake. But still — looks good. I would have been very surprised to see Charmaine with a real, pain-inflicting tattoo. If I had to choose a B word for her, it would be bewildered. A couple of new girls join us — I think their names are Margot and Gin. It's too soon to find a word for them.

We crowd into the van that will take us to camp. The air is soon filled with fragments of conversation — mostly questions having to do with Zoe.

"Tell everything," Jennifer says. "I heard she fell off a roof. What's that about? She has great balance."

I take a deep breath. I don't know how to start. Or where. The dare? The made-up kitten? The damned rooster? Jennifer is already sounding suspicious. As my father would say, she didn't just fall off a turnip truck. No, I have no idea what that means. But I do know that Jennifer already thinks Zoe is a bit over the top, and the "being the rooster" thing won't help.

"She didn't fall off the roof, exactly."

"How do you not exactly fall off a roof?" Charmaine is very literal. "Either you fall or you don't."

Jennifer nods approvingly.

I scratch my head, wondering how exactly to proceed. I could just tell the facts, but I feel I owe Zoe a better story.

"Well, you know how adventurous Zoe is," I say. They all nod. "And how curious."

"Yeah, yeah." Jennifer gestures for me to pick up the pace.

"And brave."

"Remember how she almost saved that little girl from drowning last year?" Benita offers eagerly, then she stops, as if she's remembered to be bored.

"That's right!" I say. A canoe had tipped and a ten-year-old girl was dumped into the water. Zoe was right there, in her best rescue form. The fact that the water only came up to the little girl's chest wasn't really the point.

"So?" Jennifer pushes.

"Well, Zoe was at her aunt's farm and ..." Jennifer is waiting — growing restless. I decide to go for the surefire, cute-baby-animal line. "Late one night, she thought she heard a faint mewing."

"A kitten?" Charmaine says, eyes shining.

"That's right. It was trapped on the roof of the barn and the only way Zoe could reach it was by climbing out the hayloft window. She knew it was a risk, but she had to do it, you know?"

Everyone nods, except Jennifer, who is not gullible. I feel a twinge of guilt for my embellishment. "So, anyway, she's almost reached it when the rooster crows and down she falls into the corral," I conclude in a hurry.

"What happened to the kitten?" asks Benita, missing the point somewhat.

It takes only a second. "Climbed down the side of the barn and licked her on the face!"

Everyone laughs except for Jennifer. Have I gone too far? Jennifer is not a fool, but she also doesn't have much of an imagination — no appreciation of nuance. My theory is that when you live on the Sun you don't need an imagination: you're already exactly where you want to be. You do, however, require a lot of suspicion because somebody is always trying to take your place.

"Well, that's too bad. We could have really used her on our team," Jennifer says.

"Don't you mean cabin?" I say.

"Team, cabin, whatever. You know they only accept half the CITs as counselors, right? They look at everything we do and how we do it. This is real-life stuff, Anna. Zoe was a strong competitor. We'll miss her."

And with this sympathetic statement, the van begins to move, but then halts abruptly and the door opens.

We watch as a girl enters the vehicle. The sunlight illuminates her cap of hair like she is a human color wheel. She takes the first empty seat without saying a word, but, as she pulls her backpack off, she looks straight at me and smiles.

It's not an ordinary smile. It's friendly enough — I guess it means she recognizes me from the ferry. (Maybe I wasn't as sneaky as I thought.) But there's something more in it. What's the word? It's definitely not your average, run-of-the-mill friendly smile. It is portentous — that's it: giving an omen or anticipatory sign. It bodes.

Chapter Five
Leader Chosen — No Surprises!

Big Jack greets us at the front gates. The sight of his massive frame is as familiar as the towering cedars, the weathered dock and the screaming gulls. His largeness scared me when I was nine and shy, comforted me when I was eleven and homesick and mystified me when I was thirteen and learning the butterfly stroke. He had jumped into the pool, elegantly demonstrated the demon stroke and then climbed right out again. He was surprisingly agile (and stealthy) for such a big man.

"My favorite campers," he says, as we pile out of the van. He says this to everyone, but somehow it always sounds believable.

We rush over in a swarm and take turns hugging his burly self. Most of us reach only up to the middle of his chest. His hugs are crushing and brief and feel like the official start of camp. His wife is a crusty gal (my dad's term) named Betty, who doesn't seem to want to be here. She works in the office. If you need to use the phone you have to endure a third-degree grilling about whether it's really necessary. We call her Old Betty, but not to her face.

Rainbow-girl stands on the sidelines watching the meet-and-greet-crush-hug ritual. Big Jack remarks on how we've all grown, and this year he adds that, as CITs, he's expecting us to be slightly less foolish than usual. But only slightly, he says with a wink.

"Where's your sidekick?" he asks, scanning the crowd for Zoe.

I can feel the walls of my face threaten to crumple. The sight of Big Jack and no Zoe teasing him about how he's grown makes being here too real.

"She's, uh —" I can't complete the sentence.

"Jack," Old Betty says sternly. "You remember. The camper who broke her arm?" She always calls us that — the campers. I think she'd rather we had numbers than names.

"She fell off a barn trying to rescue a kitten," Charmaine says, squeezing in beside me.

Big Jack chuckles. "That sounds like our Zoe." He opens his arms to me. "You'll be fine," he says in the voice that has soothed countless homesick or injured campers over the years.

I let myself be engulfed in his bear hug.

"Well, who have we here?" he asks.

Rainbow-girl is still standing back and looks shy. Her hands are crossed in front of her; she could be wearing a sign around her neck that says Do Not Hug. Big Jack walks up to her. She smiles up at him nervously, and then he does this courtly bow and shakes her hand. She giggles, which surprises me for some reason. She didn't seem like the giggling type beheading that daisy.

After we've registered, we schlep our stuff over to Cabin Seven. It's where we left it, huddled at the far end of the path and surrounded, almost overgrown, with lazy hollyhocks, foxgloves and a sea of buttercups. The porch slouches comfortably; its ramshackleness is like an old comfy chair that someone couldn't bear to throw out. Inside, the perfume of sea air, mold and the honeysuckle that climbs the exterior — poking fragrant faces through the open window — greets us.

"Cabin sweet cabin," Charmaine announces, throwing her arms open wide.

We choose our bunks and put away our stuff (as in cram suitcases under our beds), after which we observe a moment of silence for Zoe, our missing comrade, which only lasts ten seconds because everyone has a lot to say. Our counselor hasn't arrived — apparently she missed the boat. Jennifer seems to be happy to take over the role; she's already campaigning to be cabin leader.

"Okay," she begins. "Some of us have been here for the last bunch of years, but we also have three new people: Margot and Gin and ..." she looks questioningly to Rainbow-girl.

"Isabel," she supplies with another grin, this one not portentous at all.

"Welcome," Jennifer says. She then tells the new girls about the camp. She actually knows its history, right down to who founded it and when. I tune this out because I've heard it all before. "The most important thing you have to know ..." she is saying when I tune back in "... is that for the last three years we have lost out to Arlene Breckner's cabin in total points and, as God is my witness, this will not happen again." There's a cheer at these words, which are a complete rip-off of *Gone with the Wind*.

"But we're CITs now. Is that competition thing still on?" I ask. The competition thing has never been the highlight of my camp experience.

Jennifer looks at me as though I am a stupid younger cousin she has been ordered to play with. "There are two cabins of CIT girls. Ours and Arlene's. Of course the competition is still on. Maybe not officially, but we're still assessed on everything we do. Remember, being a counselor looks really good on your college apps."

College apps are really important to Jennifer. She already has our ten-year reunion planned and we haven't even graduated yet. She is very, very organized — one more reason why mothers everywhere just love her, even the ones who don't know her.

"Right," I say.

She smiles her forgiveness. "And the thing you new girls have to know is that we can do it, but we all need to pull together if we're going to beat Cabin Nine this year."

Again there's a cheer and, even though I feel like a total phony, I cheer along. Isabel has been silent the entire time.

"Arlene is telling everyone we don't have a chance without Zoe here," Charmaine says with a worried frown.

"Well, Arlene Breckner is a bitch, so I'm not surprised."

Margot and Gin seem taken aback by this and I feel a little sorry for them, wondering if they actually believed the camp brochure about good sportsmanship and camaraderie. Isabel's scruffy head bends slightly to the side. She raises her hand.

"Yes," Jennifer says. She is really getting into this leadership thing.

"Isn't it sort of ironic that right now in Cabin Nine this Arlene might be calling you a bitch to the new girls in there? In fact, if we had ended up in Cabin Nine, we might think you were the bitch."

A rather loud silence follows. If I were reporting, I would be tempted to call it a preternatural calm. But any way you looked at it, it was really, really quiet.

"Are you calling me a bitch?" Jennifer asks.

Isabel looks surprised. "Oh, no. I don't even know you." This doesn't help. "I just don't think there are actual people out there in the world who are just, you know, bitches. Only people who sometimes, I don't know, engage in bitchlike behavior."

I find myself smiling and I quickly pull my cheeks down with one hand like I'm massaging a facial cramp. Poor Jennifer, for all her earlier poise, looks like she's engaged in what Isabel might call confusedlike behavior. She's chewing the side of her mouth like she's missed a couple of meals.

"Can I continue?" she asks finally. It's a good call. Just move on.

"Sure," Isabel says. "I thought it was an interesting point — you know, one person's bitch is another person's best friend, maybe. No offense meant."

Jennifer out and out glares, eyes narrowed, the whole bit. "I get your point. Now why don't we go around the room and introduce ourselves ... say a couple of things to get acquainted."

Everyone goes to their bunk and sits down, all eyes naturally pointed to Jennifer who will begin — naturally.

"Well, I'm Jennifer. I'm from Vancouver. I have a 3.8 average. My interests are skiing, playing tennis and golfing with my dad, and one day I hope to be ..."

Isabel looks over to me and mouths something. I could swear it was "Miss America?" I try not to laugh.

"... Chairman of the Board." Jennifer smiles prettily and nods to Margot, who is in the bunk beside her.

Margot coughs nervously. "I'm Margot. That's spelled M-A-R-G-O-T, but you don't pronounce the T, well, duh. Anyway, I really prefer Mags. I'm from Vancouver, also."

Isabel's hand shoots up.

Margot/Mags hesitates slightly. "Yes?"

"Can I just ask you why you prefer Mags?"

A look of concern crosses Mags's face, as though she might be expecting a tirade, but Isabel waits politely.

"Well, I guess it's because I, um, don't like Margot so much. It sounds kind of stuck-up, sort of, and my ..." she flails her eyes, if this is possible, around the room, "... everybody calls me Mags."

Isabel nods. "Oh. I was just wondering because I really like the name Margot, but a person should go by the name of their choice, so Mags it is." Mags seems relieved and the introductions continue.

Benita, who is very tall, says she is not a great basketball player and has no aspirations to be a model. She tells us not to ask her how the weather is up there because it's the same and also because it is a boring question.

Charmaine says she is excited to be here, but is a little nervous about ticks and maybe getting Lyme disease.

Gin informs us that her name is short for Ginger and has nothing to do with liquor.

When it is Isabel's turn, she takes her time. She looks around the room. When she finally speaks, it is fluid. "I'm Isabel. We moved to Vancouver a year ago. I'm interested in honesty and truth and knowing what's really going on. That's about it. That's all I'm interested in."

No one speaks. It's my turn. Great. How do I follow that?

"I'm Anna," I say. "I'm from Vancouver. Normally I'm here with Zoe, but, as you all know, she's not here. And that's all." Charmaine reaches out to take my hand and I feel a little stupid, but grateful. Others murmur their sympathy.

Isabel looks at me. "Thanks, Anna. That was very enlightening." A shaft of light catches a scarlet strand of hair as she nods. I don't suppose it's possible to be taunted by a tuft of hair, is it?

Just before the bonfire and annual Big Jack talk, Jennifer pulls me aside. "She's going to be trouble."

"Who?"

"Isabel. She's not a team player. I can tell. And that's going to hurt us. Keep an eye on her, okay? See what you can find out."

"Jen, this is camp. You do remember that, don't you? It's not world domination."

Jennifer actually looks like she's considering this. Humor and Jennifer have always been on uneasy terms.

"We're supposed to have fun here," I add.

She smiles as though this is vaguely familiar. "But doing your best is fun, isn't it?"

"Right up there with ice cream and water fights."

Jennifer looks like she wants to get the joke, but then Rock-climbing guy distracts her, and she's off. Can't really blame her because he is, objectively speaking, quite hot.

I look around to see if I can spot the person who may be trouble, who may not be a team player. Isabel's sitting alone, roasting a wienie. She doesn't seem like she's really committed to it, though, because it's charred almost black. She looks like she's somewhere else.

"Hey," I say, sitting beside her. I grab a wire roaster (yesterday it was a coat hanger) and thread a wiener onto it. It's tricky — the wire has to go right down the middle of the tube or else the wiener dangles from its casing and could plummet at any moment into the fiery embers below. "Contain, refrain, explain." I hear Mr. Hong stage whisper in my ear. Okay, how's this? I try not to let the wiener fall into the fire.

"Hey," Isabel says.

"I don't think it's going to make it," I say, eyeballing her charcoal-dog.

"I like them this way."

"Burned to a crisp?"

"Well done."

"Then you're doing a fine job."

A wave of giggles comes from the general direction of Jennifer, Benita, Charmaine, Rock-climbing guy and Skater-dude. Sounds like they're having fun, but I stand (sit) my ground with Isabel. Jennifer has given me my orders and, besides, I'm a little curious about this feather-topped girl.

"You can go over there if you want," she says, without taking her eyes off her rapidly shriveling supper.

"Over where?"

Isabel smiles a you're-an-idiot smile.

"So tell me something about yourself," I say. I sound like a guidance counselor, but the words are out. There's no getting them back.

"Name, rank and serial number. That's all I'm obliged to tell you."

"Are you a prisoner of war?"

"Ooh, insightful." She smirks.

"So, why are you here? Dying to become a counselor, are you?" Sometimes the best defense is a good offense. Mr. Hong or *The Art of War*, I can't remember.

"You really want to know?"

"Sure."

"My mom vamoosed. My dad followed her out to the coast last winter, a real tear-jerking saga if you have the time. Soap-opera style. In the meantime, he has no idea what to do with a friendless teenage daughter, so voilà — camp. Here I am. Burning my wienie and bonding with you. Dad will be so happy."

"Friendless as in no friends?"

"Sharp."

"Everybody has friends."

"Okay, maybe not quite so sharp."

Mr. Hong says you can sense when there's a story in the air. He says the change is almost imperceptible except to *those with a nose*. It's acrid, he says, but just slightly. It could be the wienie, but I'm thinking there's a story here.

"What happened?" I ask.

Isabel squints one eye. And then she takes a breath. She looks into the fire.

"There was a thing."

"A thing?"

"Yeah. With Kelly and Melanie, my best friends. After which they hated each other so much they weren't speaking. Everybody else figured they had to take sides. Are you keeping up?" She turns to me.

I nod.

"So, it turns into this huge battle for, like, a year, until nobody can even remember what the 'thing' was in the first place."

She stops. More ember-watching takes place.

"And then what?"

"And then I asked Mel and Kelly if they even remembered how the whole thing started."

"And?"

"And Kelly said that Mel bought the same pants as her and Mel said that she didn't think that Kelly would mind."

"That's it?" Honestly, as a story this is a bit of a disappointment.

"Of course that's not it. That's the official reason."

"And the unofficial?'

"Like I said, you're sharp. Well, nobody would say what the unofficial one was because it's, you know, the invisible thing."

"The invisible thing?"

"Yep. There's the visible thing — the pants. And then there's the invisible thing." Isabel's supper is now a charred black finger. She shakes it off the wire and tosses it into the bowels of the fire.

"So what's the invisible thing?"

"The invisible thing was that the pants looked better on Mel, but nobody would say so. Finally I couldn't stand it anymore, so I did. I said it. And then everyone turned on me, but at least they were all together again."

"Wow," I say. "That's kind of stupid." But so true, I think. It's the kiss of death to even try on anything that might look better on you than the owner of said thing. Any fourth grader would know better.

"Yep. People are stupid. That's my theory."

I eat my hot dog while Isabel goes off to find another raw, unsuspecting wiener. As far as reporting goes, I've done okay. I've unearthed a visible thing and an invisible thing. Who knows? It may come in handy.

After we've polished off our supper, Big Jack tells us to get organized into our groups. The counselors congregate immediately, like they are magnetized. Then there are the three cabins of CITs: two female, one male. The actual campers will arrive tomorrow.

"Welcome to Camp Stillwater," he bellows. The man never uses a microphone. Sometimes at the races he uses a bullhorn. But I think he just likes the way it looks, because he doesn't need it. For the next ten minutes, he talks about the responsibility of leadership and how we are embarking on a summer of growth and maturity, cooperation and conviviality. It's your basic no-frills blah-blah-blah package. But it's Big Jack, so we pretend to listen.

Then it's time to vote for cabin leader. We talk for thirty seconds. No, that's pushing it. Charmaine suggests Jennifer; Benita seconds the motion. Jennifer pretends to be unsure, and then accepts the nomination. We vote. Jennifer wins.

At one point I look over at Isabel. I expect to see a smirk, at least. A part of me wonders if she'll object to this democratic travesty. But she's just staring into the fire. And when everybody claps and congratulates Jen, Isabel doesn't even look up.

Chapter Six
Shortcut to Soul Discovered

The cabin is soft with morning light and the purr of snoring, drooling, sputtering people in the last throes of sleep. I hear the rising wind and a couple of noisy crows. The smell of the ocean at low tide creeps in through the cracks in the walls. I can't wait to get outside. Zoe and I always — oh. She's not here. I punch my pillow and try to get comfortable again, but it's impossible. She should be here. If only she had kept her balance. If only she hadn't cared about beating a rooster.

It's such a small gap sometimes, between what happens and what should happen. Zoe should not have fallen. In that gap between standing on that beam and looking at her watch was the millisecond where she could have done something different, decided to scramble to the other side of the barn to safety. A millisecond. Downright terrifying. Conclusion: remain in bed whenever possible.

I close my eyes tightly and try to think about something that will bring back sleep, but instead I hear Mr. Hong's insistent voice. It's just a murmur, something about the reliability of my conclusion. Shut up, I think, pulling my sleeping bag up to my nose.

And then the door opens a crack, and my first thought is that Zoe is here. As if a stupid broken arm could stop the intrepid Zoe.

But a girl walks in. Correction. I can see past my lump of bedding that the creature is half-girl, half-woman. Correction on the correction. At least twenty-five percent of this being is hair — curly, out of control, push-it-out-of-the-way hair. And her face is covered with freckles, literally covered. Her eyes are enormous and brown, like maple syrup. She's not very tall and she's quite round. Okay, curvaceous — that's nicer. She's wearing loose pants, flip-flops and a T-shirt that says "Yoga, baby."

She struggles to close the door, and I'm thinking I should maybe help her, but I stay in bed. It's very warm.

Then she notices me, I guess because I'm the only one staring at her. Shoulda kept my eyes closed.

"Hi," she mouths quietly. I mime a "hello" back, but by now the others are also looking curiously at this new person who is probably our counselor.

"Hi, everybody," she says, a little louder. "I'm sorry I'm late. I missed the ferry." She looks extremely apologetic. "I'm Shell."

"As in Michelle or as in Seashell?" queries a sleepy voice from deep within her sleeping bag. Isabel. She has a thing about names, it appears.

"Just Shell."

I wait for Isabel's response. "Fine," she says as she covers her head with a pillow.

Then Jennifer notices the time and has a mini-fit — we might be late for our first breakfast, thereby costing us precious points. She starts to rouse sleepy cabinmates. Everyone responds except for Isabel.

As I'm pulling on a pair of sweats, I watch the little tableau unfold.

Shell is quietly unpacking her stuff in the corner of the room. Jennifer is standing beside Isabel's bed, trying to explain camp rules. "If we're not all there together, as in a team, we lose points."

Isabel's multi-bright head pops up from beneath her pillow. "Do we get extra points if we chew simultaneously?"

"Don't mess with me, Isabel." Her tone is icy.

Isabel sits up in bed. Her eyebrows, also dyed, fly up to frame eyes grown wide. She's about to speak when Shell says, "Hey." She has a T-shirt in either hand, which she brandishes about as she speaks. "C'mon, you guys. We can't start out this way. I'm sorry I wasn't here yesterday when everyone was being introduced. I know some of you already know each other from past years, but still, we're all in this together."

Well, she's said a whole lot of nothing as far as I can tell, but Jennifer and Isabel quietly glare at each other.

Shell continues, encouraged by the silence. "Let's just lighten up a bit. Remember what they say: Laughter is a shortcut to the soul." She looks hopeful.

Isabel's eyebrows deflate and furrow slightly. "Who are *they*?"

Shell blushes, and the effect is quite something. The color that suddenly infuses her face seems to blend all the dots together and she is now a soft peach color. She looks like a sunrise. "Well, actually, I did," she confesses.

Isabel shrugs. "Not bad."

Shell beams. She walks over to Isabel and gives her a huge hug. I stifle a laugh (even though it's a shortcut to the soul) at the look on Isabel's face. Total disbelief. She disengages herself quickly.

"Hey." She holds her hands out in front of her as Shell backs away. "Not a hugger."

Shell doesn't seem offended. She just gives a little twirl and says, "This is going to be the best summer. I can feel it."

People smile, I would say, wanly. And then there's the general thrum of Cabin Seven getting ready for the day.

I glance around the room. These are the people I will be spending my summer with. Truth is, they haven't really mattered before; it's as if they were merely a pleasant backdrop, the extras you need on a movie set. But who are they? (The verifiable facts, Mr. Hong would trumpet. Separate the facts from values.) What do I know about them?

Fact: Charmaine is afraid of ticks and heights and Jennifer, but probably not in that order. Any time she says anything, she looks at Jennifer for confirmation. That is verifiable. She has big boobs, which she hates. Also verifiable. (Direct quote: "I hate my boobs. They're too big.")

Benita is tall, with a tendency to look bored. It's hard to know if she really is bored, or if it's just a manufactured pose. The look itself goes well with her full lips, long neck and slightly heavy-lidded eyes. Maybe she took a good long look in the mirror one day and decided she might as well be what she appeared to be. This is only a theory, but verifiable, I'm sure.

Gin. Well, hard to know since I only met her yesterday. From the way she is scowling into the long, communal mirror in the corner as she fights to straighten her curly hair, I would say ... she prefers straight hair to curly. Not deep, but likely true.

Mags dislikes her name. (I can practically feel Mr. Hong rolling his eyes into the back of his head as he accuses me of not going deep enough.) Okay, okay. She is standing in front of the mirror beside Gin, and she is trying to pop an invisible zit. She is complaining about her skin, which appears to be nearly perfect. She could be complaining about her nose (which is large), but she is not. No conclusion available.

Jennifer, aside from being polite, poised, etc., hates it when things are done the wrong way — that is, not her way. (My proof for this dates back to the eighth grade when Zoe and I were painting a poster for a school dance. She said the green we chose didn't look like springtime grass and it should because it was a spring dance. What were we thinking? I'm not kidding.) She doesn't laugh a whole lot (also provable) and she doesn't like it when people call her Jen. She requires every one of her three syllables.

Then there's Isabel. If I were writing any of this down, this is probably where I would run out of ink. If we were playing poker, she would be the wild card. If she were a weather pattern, she'd probably be a hailstorm. If … Mr. Hong were here, he'd be rolling his eyes again and reminding me of something he made me memorize. "We shall give an accurate picture of the world … wherever human nature or real life displays its freaks and vagaries." I have an uneasy feeling that Isabel might be a freak — maybe a vagary — but I can't prove this.

Once Jennifer is ready, she stands beside the door and does an official countdown for time remaining before first bell — the warning gong that signals breakfast. Isabel mutters something about how it's like camping with Dick Clark on New Year's Eve, but either Jennifer doesn't hear or has chosen to respond to Isabel only when necessary or doesn't know who Dick Clark is.

Outside the cabin, Jennifer pulls me aside. "Will you wait and make sure that Isabel gets there on time?"

"Me? Why me?"

Jennifer's expression turns Chairman-of-the-Boardish. "Because you're nice and you get along with everybody."

I try to think of a comeback, but it's hard to combat this statement. I do tend to get along with everybody and I am pretty nice. "But I don't want to." When in doubt, whine.

"Anna." Jennifer tilts her head. "If we don't show up on time, we —"

"I know, I know." I throw up my hands. "We lose points."

"You know how much Zoe wanted to beat Arlene this year."

Oh, playing the Zoe card is so unfair.

And so effective.

I trudge back into the cabin. Isabel is still dressed in her pajama bottoms and T-shirt. She's reading a book and looking very relaxed. As though she is on vacation. Or at camp.

I wander casually over to my bunk, where I rummage through my backpack pretending to look for something — something I needed desperately enough to bring me back here. But what? A pen? No. Lip gloss? A possibility. Insect repellent? Better. Pocket knife? Perfect.

I find my little knife and hold it aloft briefly. "There you are," I say before plopping it into my pocket. When I turn around, Isabel is watching me.

"That was a perfect soap-opera moment," she says,

leaning back on her pillow so that bright colors are splayed against white cotton, making her look like a very smug peacock.

"What do you mean?"

She flips her legs over the side of her bed and pushes a sprig of lemon-colored hair out of her face. "It's kind of like the speeches that soap-opera characters burst into when they're completely alone. You know —" Isabel presses her hands together and begins to wring them. "I shall wait until morning and then get my revenge. All of Port Charles will know my name, Monique de …" She smirks. "… de whatever."

"I don't know what you're talking about."

Isabel smirks deeper, if that's possible, and points a lazy finger. "That's another one! Feigning ignorance. Although it was more convincing, actually."

"I really don't —" I begin, but she stops me with a look.

"Jennifer sent you back in here to get me because she doesn't want to lose cabin points. You didn't want to come."

I consider denying the allegations, but she has this very intense look about her that makes lying seem like a bad idea. Some people are very easy to lie to because they don't look you directly in the eyes. It's easier to lie to a nose or an ear. I don't know why, but it is. Isabel's eyes, which are flecked with gold and burgundy, didn't spare you. "How did you know?"

She shrugs. "I'm really perceptive and aware and, you know, conscious."

"Hmm."

"And you and Jennifer were standing beside the window."

Ah, the old standing-beside-the-window trick. Subtract ten detective points for me. "So, are you coming or not?" I grumble as I move to the door.

She shuffles into a pair of sandals, runs a hand through her spiky hair and joins me, still wearing pajama bottoms. "I could eat," she says as first bell rings.

I try to move the pace along once we're outside, but this Isabel person will not be rushed. She's stretching her arms, taking deep breaths and, in general, communing with nature. I'm looking at my watch and thinking that Jennifer will kill me if I don't deliver Isabel on time.

I'm also thinking wistfully that if Zoe was here, none of this would be happening. We would be eating pancakes by now.

"What are you scowling about?" Isabel asks.

"Nothing."

"One should always scowl at something. It's a waste of a good scowl to scowl at nothing. Scowl. Now that's a funny word, isn't it? The more you say it, the more ludicrous it sounds —"

"We should move a little quicker."

If anything, Isabel slows down, but we squeak in under the wire, or bell in this case. As we slide onto the bench, Jennifer gives me a look that's half approval, half concern.

Shell and Gin go to fetch the bacon and eggs. While they're gone, Jennifer leans over to Benita and stage whispers, "There she is."

I look over my shoulder. Arlene Breckner has arrived. She is, as they say, a fine figure of a woman. Or at least of an almost-woman. She's tall and sleek and really quite nice, but freakishly athletic and therefore the bane of our lives, almost always coming first in the annual swimming race. Zoe beat her last year by a nose. (Arlene had a fever of 102, but we don't talk about that.) I placed a respectable third.

"Who?" Isabel stage whispers back.

"Arlene Breckner," Charmaine states as though this should be obvious.

"The bitch?" Isabel says in a regular voice.

Jennifer's head snaps toward Isabel and something like a smile, but not a smile, creeps over her face. "Um, Isabel?"

"Yes, Jennifer?"

"I don't know you very well," she begins.

"Nor I you," Isabel responds.

Another smile-like configuration breaks out on Jennifer's face. "Could you be quiet for, like, a second?"

"I could try," Isabel says seriously. "For the team."

Jennifer's eyes narrow. "It's just that we get ten points knocked off of our total score for cursing."

Isabel leans her head to one side. "But that's what you called her last night."

Jennifer sighs. "That was in private."

"Okay. So, no public cursing? Gotcha. Does this edict include any kind of cursing?"

Jennifer nods, but suspiciously.

"Like, for example, if I said 'zounds,' or 'egad,' or 'criminy'?"

"Or 'gadzooks'?" I add without thinking. I regret this impulsive action immediately.

But Isabel is nodding happily. " 'Gadzooks' is an excellent example."

"I think you know what I mean," Jennifer says sternly. "No swearing period, okay?"

Isabel puts a hand to her chest. "I'll do my best."

"I just want to make sure that we're all together, you guys." Jennifer looks around the table. "Because if we don't stand together, we fall apart."

The others give a small cheer. All I can muster is a feeble yet encouraging (I hope) smile because I've heard this line for the last three years and, to tell you the truth, it never impressed me that much even in the beginning.

Isabel snickers.

"What are you laughing at?" Jennifer asks.

"It's just a reaction that I have when I notice that the emperor, or empress in this case, has no clothes."

I'm almost sure I can see Jennifer counting to ten. She gives me a little glance that says, See what I mean?

It is a little nervy for Isabel to throw out comments about clothes — even if it is only metaphorically — when she herself is wearing only pajamas, but I say nothing. Jennifer simmers, Isabel grins and then Shell and Gin are back with breakfast.

"Bon appetit," Shell announces to a very quiet table. "Good food is fuel for the soul," she adds, but immediately frowns and sits down.

Cleanup is a big part of the CIT's job description, so after breakfast I find myself in the recycling bin — not exactly in, but close enough. I'm separating bottles from cans, when Big Jack appears. He is surprisingly quiet for such a big man, almost like Jiminy Cricket — if Jiminy Cricket were almost seven feet tall.

"Best part of the day, hmm?"

"You know it," I say. "I especially enjoy it when people jam the straws down the necks of the bottles. It's a great challenge." I try to coax one out with little success.

"Well, that's the real reason you're here," he says. "The other stuff is just a time-filler." He lowers his largeness and sits beside me. In his other life he is a businessman, I think, but really I can't imagine him anywhere but camp.

"So, how's it going without your good buddy?"

"It's a little weird," I say, giving up on the straw and going back to separating bottles and cans.

"Change is tough. But you'll make new friends, get to know the old ones a little better. You get along well with people."

"Yeah, I guess."

"That's the spirit," he chuckles.

"The *sprit.*"

"What's that?"

"Nothing. It's just … it feels weird without her. Like something's missing, you know? Like my arm or my leg. Or my head."

"Sure. She *is* missing. I guess I've gotten used to people coming and going. I've been doing this for more than fifteen years, you know."

"My entire life."

He groans. "That doesn't make me feel old. You know what always surprises me?"

I don't say anything because I recognize Big Jack's rhetorical take-a-moment-to-impart-wisdom tone. I don't mind.

"All the people I've watched come and go through this place — everyone always thinks they're the star."

"Huh?"

"It's true. Some people don't act like it — some are shy, others act like they're too small to be noticed — but deep down everybody always thinks they're the main character of the story. And the truth is, I think, that we're all just part of the same story. Nobody's more important than anyone else."

"Huh," I say again because I can't think of anything else. I'm not sure I agree. Some people definitely seem more important than others. Queens and prime ministers. Rock stars. Arlene Breckner, Jennifer, Zoe — bigger somehow, more important.

"Well, that's just what I think," he shrugs. "I better get going. The sink's plugged and it ain't gonna get unplugged on its own. That's how important I am."

As he leaves, he walks past the faucet. He turns the water on and brings the hose back to me. For a second I think he's going to spray me, and I think, that's weird, but then he takes a bottle from my hand. He lets the water trickle inside and soon the straw is bobbing to the top. "Sometimes you just have to try something new," he says.

"I would have figured that out," I shout to his retreating back. He just raises a hand and keeps moving.

Just outside the cabin, Isabel walks up to me. "Hey, about this morning — how come you didn't say anything?"

"What are you talking about?"

"About me wearing pajamas. When I said the emperor's new clothes thing? You looked right at them — I read your mind."

"Yeah, right. You don't even know me."

"Sure I do." She shrugs.

"No, you don't."

"Yeah, I do." She smiles at me. "You're the girl who 'gets along.' You're the smartest girl in the class who'd die before she let anybody find out. You're the girl nobody hates." She runs her hand through her unruly mop and shrugs her thin shoulders. "And I'm the girl everybody hates. Ain't life funny?"

Then she just walks away in her floppy little pajamas and her tousled head of hair, and I try to figure out if I've been insulted.

The campers have arrived, and they stream around me like I'm an upright log in a river. I watch them scream and push and laugh their way to their cabins. I watch their shortness and their excitement. Some are tentative and some are fearless. I remember these first days. How important it was to find your place and hold onto it. Grab a bunk, a friend, a corner for your own. Survival.

Isabel's words ring in my ears. It wasn't my fault if people liked me, was it? Ever since kindergarten kids have liked me. In the intermediate years, when Top Five lists showed up, kids still liked me. I was always in the top five. Top Five Girls You'd Like to Be Friends With. Top Five Most Popular. Top Five Prettiest. Even the Top Five You'd Like to Spend the Rest of Your Life With. (That was seventh grade.) I always made top five. Never number one, of course. That was too dangerous. (Number one girls tended to be toppled by number two girls.)

The only list I never made was the Top Five Girls You Hate. Never. Not once.

Chapter Seven
Colorful Girl Fears Snotgreen Sea

Camp Stillwater is a water camp. Kayaking, swimming, diving, sailing — basically if it gets you wet, it's a Camp Stillwater activity. So when Isabel tells me that she is afraid of the water, this strikes me as significant.

We're on our way down to the beach, where we'll be classified according to our swimming abilities. I will be a Shark, the top category, as I have been for the last few years. And since one of the things about being a CIT is to assist in one of the programs, I'm hoping I'll be put in something that requires I be in, not just near, the water. I love the water. Plus, I could work on my tan. Win–win situation.

"How afraid?" I ask.

"I have no trouble drinking it."

"Really, Isabel. How scared are you?"

"I'm not scared," she says indignantly. "I'm afraid."

"Okay. What's the difference?"

"The difference is that one I am and one I am not."

"Okay."

"Stuff that I'm scared of, I don't back away from. Being afraid of something — truly afraid — is different. You need to respect it and wait for it. You can't force it. Aren't you afraid of anything?"

Only this conversation. "Look! The ocean," I say.

"Good segue."

The water shimmers. It glints, flirts and winks up at us, completely aware of its power. Or maybe not — who knows? Zoe and I would already have run down the slope and plunged in with blood-curdling shrieks. I can see us. There we are, swimming out to the buoy and pretending he's tall and dark and handsome. And funny.

"The snotgreen sea. The scrotumtightening sea," says Isabel.

"I beg your pardon?"

"James Joyce. *Ulysses.*"

"Well, that's just lovely." I shrug off my towel and the ugly quote and run down the embankment to the shore.

I get my swimming test over with quickly. It's just a formality. Drip, the head swimming coach, gives me a smiling thumbs-up when I climb onto the wharf. "Go see Karim for your assignment," she calls.

I grab my towel and dry off the best I can. Isabel is still standing where I left her. She is huddled in her sweatpants and an oversized sweatshirt. I know she has a bathing suit on under there, but it's impossible to tell.

"You looked great," she says. "You're an awesome swimmer."

I try to look modest. "I have to go see Karim. Are you going in or not?"

She scrunches up her face. "I don't know."

I look at her, and then I look at the ocean. It's practically flat today, a soft purple. It looks like a giant bathtub to me. I lean into Isabel. "Personally, I don't think there's that much difference between being scared and being afraid."

I can't read her face. I nudge her in the side. "You can do it. Just try floating. They love floaters here."

"I don't float," she says.

When I get to the top of the hill, I look back to see if she's made any progress. She hasn't. The wind flips her colorful hair around her face and the sun illuminates the fire-engine red bits so she looks like a signal fire on the beach. Jennifer, Charmaine and Mags whip past her and I see that Jennifer stops to get her to join them. I can't hear Isabel's response, but I see Jennifer's disapproving face as they charge toward the water. Isabel still doesn't move. Who doesn't float?

As I walk to the pool, the loss of Zoe hits me just below my rib cage. If she were here she'd be a Shark, too. Maybe we'd both get the same assignment. It's what we had requested on our registration sheet: swimming/coaching duty.

I walk through the gates and search for Karim. He used to be the junior lifeguard and swimming coach, and before that he'd been a camper here. He was an amazing swimmer — Olympic hopeful. Last year he kept yelling at me to demand more from myself. I grew quite tired of him. He was way too pushy and way too full of himself. I was actually surprised to hear that he was back. I'd have thought he'd be in serious Olympic training.

He's standing on the pool deck, and when he sees me, he waves me over to him.

Something has happened to Karim. Since last year he has turned gorgeous. Objectively, I try to figure out what's changed. Same deep brown eyes, same toffee-colored skin, same strong swimmer's build and black, silky hair that would brush the top of his shirt collar, if he wore a shirt, which would be a shame.

Nothing has really changed, yet my pulse has increased. I don't remember this happening last year. I do remember my mother asking me why I'd never written about him when she picked me up from the ferry. Why would I? I'd responded.

Now all I can think is he is totally worth writing home about. He is what Zoe and I would call a *mentionable*. I stop for a second to reapply my watermelon lip gloss. My lips are dry, no big deal.

"McKay," he says. It's in the same voice except I don't remember it sounding like warm caramel on ice cream, and I don't remember it having the power to render me stupid.

"Hey," I say, relieved at how cool I sound. I nod as I say this, but maybe for too long because I find that

I'm still nodding even after my one-syllable answer has slipped into the growing silence. I'm pretty sure I look like one of those wobbly-headed dogs you see in the backs of cars.

He asks about Zoe. I give him the shortened version of her mishap because, as we're speaking, his full, seductive lips seriously handicap my concentration. Then I realize he's asked me something. "Uh, pardon? I didn't catch the last part," I say, quite cleverly.

"How does that sound?"

"Oh." Crap. How does what sound? I quickly examine his body language to see if it will tell me something, like maybe if he's just suggested a walk on the beach at midnight. He crosses his arms in front of him and waits. He doesn't really look that friendly. Probably not the beach thing. Probably something else. "Um, sounds fine," I say.

"Okay. I actually asked for Zoe. I didn't realize she broke her arm. It's too bad. She's a hard worker."

"Yeah, right, she is." I cross my arms as well. "Huh?"

"Huh, what?"

"Huh, hum, you asked for Zoe?"

He looks down at the ground, sighs, then looks up again. "To be my assistant? I thought she showed a lot of potential last year." He peers deeply into my eyes, which would be romantic except that I'm pretty sure he's checking to see if there's a pharmaceutical reason for my stupidity.

"Right. Assistant. So I'm your second choice?" I say this quite coyly. Because these are the signals I'm getting from Karim? Because this would be the right course of action? No. I say this because I'm an idiot.

Karim looks like he wants to be somewhere else. "Well, Arlene is going to be working with Drip. So …"

Okay, so I'm actually third choice. "The kids are arriving," he adds. I nod. I've never been so thrilled to hear the sound of screaming children in my life.

They arrive in a throng. Behind them is Isabel. Her sweat suit is gone and her towel is wrapped around her waist like a sarong. She's wearing sunglasses. She looks glamorous, in an off-kilter way.

"What are you doing here?" I mouth while Karim takes the names of the new kid shipment.

She slips her glasses down the bridge of her nose and peers over them. "Learning to swim," she mouths back.

I can't keep the surprise off of my face because she's a little old for this group, but I immediately adjust my face from a "what the?" contortion to a "that's cool" expression.

Isabel laughs at my attempt, which kind of ticks me off. You'd think that someone surrounded by munchkins would be a little more humble.

"Are you the counselor?" Karim asks Isabel.

"Counselor in training," she says. "I'm here for swimming lessons."

"But you're so big." A little girl with red curls blurts out what we are all thinking.

"Only in size," Isabel says, taking off her glasses. "I'm afraid of the water," she says to Karim. "Personally I think that if we were meant to swim we would have been born with webbing between our fingers and toes, but that's just me. I'm into facing my fears these days so that's why I'm here. I tried dipping my toe into the ocean because someone suggested it, but I was completely unsuccessful."

Karim just nods and says, "Everybody's afraid of something. How are you with pools?"

"I'm good with the shallow end," she says. Her voice is less Princess-of-the-Nile now.

I'm a little surprised at Karim's response. Last year he was always on my back to push forward, push through, push myself out of the way (whatever that meant). A lot of talk about pushing, that's all I remember.

"McKay, in the pool." He barks me out of my thoughts and into the present. Yup, this is the Karim I remember.

I join the throng of Lilliputians and Isabel in the shallow end. If I were Isabel I would be mortified, but she looks more concerned about the H_2O than public opinion. I paddle over. "How are you doing?" I whisper.

She seems surprised to see me, as though she can't remember why I would be here. Her eyes are hollow and her lips are a very faint shade of aquamarine. Her teeth are chattering even though it's a warm day and the pool is protected from the ocean breezes by a tall fence. "I've been better."

Karim swims over. "You don't have to do this unless you're helping the kids with the water sports, you know," he says to Isabel.

"Uh, no, that's okay," she says, still shivering. "I want to get over this."

"Good for you. That's awesome." He says this in a friendly way. But then he turns to me. "Go over and help the kids with the kickboards. I'll help Isabel."

I paddle away. I'm immediately swarmed by kids — a popsicle stick covered with ants. But even amid the tangled confusion, I manage to watch Karim and Isabel. He holds her hands as he leads her into waist-deep water. He's watching her, but she's looking down at the water. When they hit the drop-off point by the rope, Karim says something and she laughs. It's a very pretty sound and she looks very pretty making it, and then he laughs, too, and the whole scene is so pretty that I want to puke with jealousy. This surprises me.

"Hey, miss," a little kid calls out to me.

"What?" I say, practically growling. Then I notice that the little red-haired waif has floated out beyond the drop-off line and is barely clinging to the swimming board.

Karim and I get there at the same time. I can tell by the look on his face that he's pissed at me, but then he's using the same reassuring tone with the little floating girl that he used with Isabel. As he pulls the girl back to the safe harbor of the shallow end, she giggles even while he's warning her about not going beyond the roped-off zone. It seems he can be charming when he wants to be.

I'm very diligent for the rest of the class, but when it's over and everyone leaves the pool, Karim asks me to stay. He doesn't say anything right away. He rubs a towel over his hair and puts on a T-shirt quite leisurely. Maybe he isn't too mad. "I guess this wasn't a good idea after all," he says.

At first I don't know what he means, and then it hits me that I may have been fired just slightly less than an hour from the time I was hired. "What?" I squawk.

"When you're working with kids, you have to be responsible and conscientious. All it takes is a second for them to slip under the water and drown. It would be tough to explain to a parent that their kid died because my assistant was putting on lip gloss."

"That's so unfair. I wasn't putting on lip gloss. In the pool."

"It doesn't matter what you were doing. You weren't paying attention. As far as I'm concerned, camp is for the campers, not the counselors. It's just good policy to keep them alive. I'm sorry, McKay. We'll find something else for you to do."

His face is one cold, hard slab and he sounds so arrogant that I want to scream, but I know this won't help, so I take a deep breath. What I know for sure is that I really want to be assistant coach. In a summer that already looks crappy, this would be a bright light. He starts to walk away, but I follow him.

"I didn't even know an hour ago that I was going to be doing this! You didn't give me a whole lot of warning, just 'Get in the pool.'" I mimic his bossy voice and this gives me a bit of pleasure. "I think you owe me another chance."

He turns around. "I owe you another chance?" He squints one eye because of the sun, and probably because he knows how attractive it makes him look, but I'm having absolutely none of this because I officially ended my crush about the same time he accused me of putting on lip gloss in the pool. Who wears waterproof lip gloss, anyway?

"Yes," I say, and then, for good measure, "I believe you do."

His mouth scrunches up and then relaxes. "Well, that's as gutsy as I've ever seen you, so okay. You get one more chance, but if I catch you so much as checking out a fingernail during practice, you are out. Understand?"

I nod because I don't want to say anything that might get me assigned to a truly heinous duty. (Last year one CIT spent the entire summer cleaning toilets.)

I grab my towel and walk off in what I hope is a dignified manner, although it's hard to be dignified when you're wearing a wet bathing suit that's seeping through the bum of your sweatpants. Still, I probably pull it off. But, as I'm walking back to the cabin, the words "that's as gutsy as I've ever seen you" bash around in my head and make me mad. How come he thinks he knows me? Because he's seen me swim a few times over the last couple of years? Because, what, he's such a great reader of character? The whole thing makes me wriggle inside my skin. Who does he think he is?

That's when I turn my walk into a run because this boy has me thinking in stupid, ordinary phrases like "Who does he think he is?"

Argh. This would never have happened if Zoe was here.

Objective conclusion: Day: bad. Karim: jerk.

Chapter Eight
Goose Cooked —
Well Done

I tell Charmaine and Benita about how unjust Karim was as we walk to the barbecue pit for dinner. Charmaine is very sympathetic and Benita actually seems moderately interested. They both agree that he was way out of line, but quite handsome.

I argue that his looks are completely irrelevant, not to mention at odds with his personality. He is demanding, harsh and judgmental. And what was that "gutsy" crack about anyway?

"You are really good with words," Charmaine says, when I finally finish railing.

"Thank you," I say, mollified somewhat.

"Anna, can I talk to you?" Jennifer appears out of nowhere.

Benita and Charmaine continue to the pit.

"Sure," I say, as Jennifer pulls me over to a tree in a manner usually seen in bad spy movies.

"Well, we're cooked now," she states.

"We're what?"

"Cooked. As in our goose is."

"What happened?"

"I don't know where to start. Arlene Breckner is in the best shape of her entire life. Did you know she runs every morning at five thirty?" She states this in a crescendo, but lowers her voice quickly, keeping with her B spy-movie status. "Five thirty?"

"Well, she's usually in good shape, and she always wins the big race, so what's new? There's other stuff we do well. You're awesome at sailing and archery."

Jennifer looks slightly appeased at the mention of her abilities. "That's true," she acknowledges. "And Char and Benita are good at diving, and Mags is supposedly pretty good in a kayak."

"So then?"

"Well, that's all before the Isabel factor."

"The Isabel factor?"

"Yes. She's changing everything. We've already lost points because of her. She doesn't make her bed —"

I gasp.

Jennifer frowns. "She doesn't make it to meals on time."

"When has she been late?"

"Today at lunch. And she says every little thing that she's thinking! It's like she doesn't care about the rules!" She says this totally seriously. "We have to nip this thing in the bud!"

"Maybe we should wait and see how it goes before we do any nipping. Besides, is winning the race that important? I mean, it's not like we're just campers anymore, and camp really is for the —" I stop myself before I quote Karim completely. "Maybe we should be focusing on other stuff."

Jennifer stares at me as though I've lost my mind. "Everything counts, Anna. They assess our ability to work as a team as well as the races, and we can't let Arlene win, not after we beat her last year! Zoe would never give up."

"I'm not giving up," I say, once again seduced by the Zoe card.

"Then help me," she says. "Isabel seems to like you, as much as she likes anyone. She talks to you."

"So?"

"So, you can keep her in line. Get her to see how important this is."

"Why?"

"Why what?"

"Why is this so important?"

Jennifer looks mystified, and I suddenly realize that "Why?" is probably rarely asked of people who live on the Sun. They're probably more concerned with "How?" — as in "How do I stay where I am?"

"Never mind," I say.

"Just keep an eye on her, okay? Or keep her out of the way."

I nod and say I will even though I have a very weird feeling in the pit of my stomach. Mr. Hong would say that you should always listen to your gut. But you know what? At this moment, Mr. Hong is on a beach in Hawaii drinking blender drinks. Maybe I needed to stop listening to his absentee advice.

After two hot dogs the uneasiness goes away and I think that maybe my gut was just telling me I was hungry. But then Isabel shows up and I feel weird again.

"You're late," Jennifer barks, mustard escaping from the side of her mouth in a bubble, giving her a slightly insane appearance.

"I had a phone call," she says. She sits down beside me.

"Someone from home?" Shell asks, nibbling on a carrot. She has forsworn the meat because of its "truly heinous contents," the bun because of the white flour, known as "white death," and the ketchup due to the high sugar content, also known as "white death." As a result, her plate is covered with celery and carrots and looks pretty pitiful.

Isabel shrugs and digs into her hot dog. She has forsworn nothing and her dinner is piled high with onions, sauerkraut, mushrooms and who knows what else. Maybe it's my imagination, but it seems that Shell is watching Isabel's hot dog longingly.

"You know, one hot dog isn't going to kill you," Isabel says.

Shell straightens. "I know. And I don't want to get in the way of your enjoyment. I mean, pleasure is, you know, worth something, too. It's just my choice, my decision. I'm not judging anyone," she says.

"Okay," Isabel says, stuffing the last of her hot dog into her mouth. It barely fits.

"You know, I was thinking," Shell says suddenly, tearing her eyes away from our meals. "Wouldn't it be fun to start the day with a yoga session?"

Her tone makes it sound like she's just suggested hot fudge sundaes and cute firemen. Her actual words get an identical response from everyone. Complete silence.

"It would be fun," she continues. "And it would get everyone centered and connected and focused …" She looks around the circle for any sign of encouragement or even life. "And toned," she adds.

Jennifer perks up at this. "Is it good for physical fitness?"

"Absolutely. And for concentration."

I can see the wheels turning in Jennifer's brain.

"Would we get extra cabin points for initiative?"

Shell looks stymied. "I don't know. I could ask."

"Well, Arlene Breckner's cabin is getting extra points for their five thirty a.m. runs, so we should get extra points for this."

Isabel snorts at the mention of Arlene Breckner, but doesn't say anything.

"I could ask," Shell says quickly.

"I'll come with you." Jennifer stands up immediately.

"Now?" Shell says. "Oh, well, no time like the present, I guess." She stands as well, wiping bark and dirt off her pants. "It's, it's …" Almost immediately she is stumped. "My energy must be really blocked."

"Maybe you need more nitrites," Isabel suggests. Shell doesn't respond, but I think I see her shoulders stiffen as she walks away. It's quite something to get on the nerves of someone who is entirely dedicated to inner peace and tranquility.

"So," says Isabel, "what did Karim want with you after swimming practice?"

I launch into the story, leaving out nothing. He was unfair, I say, authoritarian, practically a despot, out only for his own power-mongering ways, possibly wanting complete control of the swimming program for some nefarious and evil purpose. I have to stop talking because I'm out of breath.

Isabel looks thoughtful, as in full of thought. Not a good sign. "It *is* a pretty serious responsibility watching out for kids in water."

Long pointed needle: Isabel.

Big red balloon: me.

Chapter Nine
CIT Renamed

I barely eat my breakfast the next morning. First of all, it's porridge, so — gross. Second, I have swimming with the Bottom-feeders first thing and I am a little nervous about seeing Karim, especially since I've been forced to reevaluate his beastliness due to Isabel's unfortunate rightness.

I decide to go over a little early to make a good second impression.

The pool is empty; the water is bright aquamarine and mirror-smooth. The faint smell of chlorine mixes with the early-morning ocean smells drifting in from the beach. It must be eighty degrees already and it isn't even ten o'clock. I'm thinking about sneaking a swim, when Karim walks up behind me.

"Go ahead," he says, reading my mind. "The kids won't be here for twenty minutes or so."

Suddenly I feel uncomfortable, as though I've sprouted chin hairs, a third eye and a second nose. "Are you sure?"

"I wouldn't have said it if I didn't mean it."

I peel off my T-shirt and walk to the end of the pool. All my good intentions about getting along, being cooperative and pleasant are rapidly disappearing.

I break the skim of calm with my arms and I know it's a perfect dive. It's hard to figure out how things have gone wrong in an imperfect dive — someone has to tell you — but a perfect dive just feels right. I swim ten lengths with barely a break in my turns. With every lap I feel stronger, as though life is being breathed into me. My mind is locked onto one single thought: "I will not let him get to me. I will not let him get to me." With each stroke — three before I breathe — I find myself chanting "I ... will ... not."

When I finally climb out of the pool, I'm breathless but exhilarated. I've lost track of the time and the number of lengths, and I'm as calm as a Buddha. I can face anything now, even beastly Karim. I walk past him to get to my towel and clothes.

"Why don't you swim like that all the time?" he asks, looking down at his stopwatch.

"You were timing me?"

"Just the first twenty laps, then you eased up. You're in decent shape this year."

I feel my face turn red.

"Sometimes you're lazy, but that was nice."

Kids start filing in, which is good because I might have gotten all mad about the lazy dig, and that's really not the path you want to take when you're trying to make a good second impression. Why, again, was I trying to do this?

At the shallow end of the pool, Karim instantly morphs into friendly, charming swimming coach. I wave to Isabel, who is at the end of the line making friends with her fellow Bottom-feeders. It seems they've grown used to having a giant among them.

"Hey, Gulliver," I whisper, as I sidle up beside her.

"How did it go with Karim this morning?" she whispers back.

"McKay, if you're not too busy, could you come up here and meet the kids?"

"Coming," I call out. To Isabel, I whisper, "Swell, if you don't count his mood swings."

"And this is my assistant, Anna," Karim says as I approach.

"Anna Banana." A little girl who I instantly dislike shouts out that much-despised name. I muster up a fake smile.

Karim smiles back. "Okay with you, Anna?"

I have obviously missed something, but I'm in no mood to admit it. "Sure," I nod.

"Anna Banana, Anna Banana," they begin chanting.

Finally I can't hide my confusion. "Huh?" I say to Karim, who is now grinning with his cursed straight, white teeth.

"Nicknames," he says. "We were trying to come up with a nickname for you. And since you've agreed, Anna Banana you will be henceforth."

I quietly fume as Karim describes pool rules and etiquette. Apparently making fun of one's assistant is a breach of nothing. When he dismisses the kids to retrieve the kickboards, I ask, "So, what's your nickname?"

"Water boy," he says.

"Hmm. Maybe mine should have something to do with water as well?"

"I like Anna Banana," he says. "It suits you." Then he smiles, but because he is wearing his nasty cop-who-is-taking-bribes sunglasses, I can't see where he's looking. But I will not give him any satisfaction by reacting, so I walk away and help the kids with their boards.

I manage not to drown any of my charges, and I even have their names memorized by the end of the hour. They've all taken to my new moniker with gusto; some, in their enthusiasm, have shortened it simply to Banana.

Karim spends quite a bit of time with Isabel, which I note only for purely professional reasons. Surely the campers deserve as much attention? At the end of the class, when everyone has left the pool area, I point this out in my most neutral, swimming-assistant voice.

"Are you jealous?" is his reply.

I then do something that I'm actually quite proud of: I don't say a word. I turn and walk away. Mostly I do it because I can't think of anything to say, but later I decide that it will have made the perfect impression.

When I'm dressed, I wander over to the tuck shop, buy a bag of licorice and head over to the big fir tree that Big Jack has dubbed the Honesty Tree. When I see Isabel sitting there among its jutting roots, I feel a little shiver of apprehension. Isabel doesn't need an Honesty Tree.

"Hey," she calls out.

I sit down in the grass across from her and offer my bag of licorice. She takes one with a smile.

"Thanks, Anna Banana."

I glower. "Do not —"

"Okay," she says. "But it's not that bad."

"Yes, it is. What kind of perverse pleasure do you think he gets from humiliating me?"

Isabel winds her licorice around her finger and actually appears to be holding back an opinion.

"What?" I press.

She looks around furtively. "Did I say something?"

"You didn't say something quite loudly."

"Oh."

"So, tell me."

"The real question is, Why do you care?"

"I don't care."

Isabel gives me a one-eyebrow-raised look, which requires a dexterity I would admire on another day.

"Yeah, you do — because you like him."

"I do not," I say quietly, hoping she will lower her voice. "You are so wrong."

"I am never wrong."

"You are never wrong?" I ask because I think she's just said she's never wrong. "Never? Never wrong?"

She smiles. "Yup. About this kind of thing. I don't go in for don't-say-what-you-mean kinds of feelings, so it makes no difference to me one way or the other. I'm completely objective and that's why I'm never wrong. I can't be. I don't care about the outcome."

I'm still feeling irritated by this remarkable statement when Arlene Breckner and Jennifer walk by, chatting and laughing. Hands are flapping, hair is flipping; things are quite animated. To the casual observer, this would appear to be friendly behavior. Arlene is wearing a sports bra and a pair of shorts that reveal long, taut legs. In military terms, you could bounce a quarter off those quads.

When Jennifer looks up and sees Isabel and me, she halts. I can almost see the late-breaking news bulletin cross her forehead: Retreat, retreat.

But Isabel leans forward and waves for them to join us. Jennifer puts on a brave little soldier expression and guides Arlene (who can only be guided, not led) our way.

"Hi, guys," Jennifer says, very cheerfully.

Isabel and I say hi.

"Arlene, this is Isabel — she's new this year. And you know Anna, of course."

Arlene smiles at Isabel and then squints one eye at me. I squint back. "So, Zoe isn't here this year."

I get the feeling that the edges are blurring

around us and that we are facing each other on a dusty road in the middle of a dustier town, both reaching for our pistols (or, in this case, our nose plugs and swimming caps). "Yep," I say, totally into character and wishing I chewed tobacco.

"So you're the famous Arlene," Isabel drawls. It's almost as if she knows the fantasy that is playing inside my head. "You know there's only room in this town for one swimming champion."

Jennifer giggles nervously and Arlene chuckles, mostly looking and sounding like she's not into this western motif at all. She looks past Isabel to me. "I hear you're working with Karim this summer."

I nod and make a slashing gesture across my throat to Isabel in case she wishes to speak further, but, because Arlene is looking at me, I have to be subtle and succeed only in pressing my finger to my throat as though I've sprung a leak. "Yeah," I say kind of choked because of the finger on my throat. "We're working with the ten and unders."

"The Bottom-feeders," Arlene clarifies.

"My alma mater," Isabel volunteers.

"Your what? As in you used to be?"

Isabel shakes her head. "As in I presently am. I'm not much of a swimmer. Not like Anna. She's going to be hard to beat this year."

I am horrified. Challenging Arlene Breckner is like holding a piece of raw meat out to a mastiff tied to his doghouse by a single hair.

Arlene gives us a slow, gunslinger smile. "Well, it's all

fun," she says, and then walks over to a group of Cabin Nine girls who have gathered yonder.

Jennifer has been freakishly silent during this whole exchange, but when Arlene is out of earshot, she hisses at Isabel, "What was that about?"

Isabel actually looks a little thrown off by this. "What?"

"Telling Arlene that Anna is the one to beat?"

"It's a surprise?"

But Jennifer throws up her hands in disgust. "You explain to her," she says to me.

"All I've heard about since I got here is this big competition between Cabin Seven and Cabin Nine and the big, final race. Suddenly it's a secret?"

"It's not a secret," I try to explain. "It's just a, you know, friendly competition."

Isabel leans to one side and taps her head with her hand. The symbolism is quite clear.

Jennifer gets up with a groan. "Don't knock too hard. What's left of your brain might fall out." And then she flounces off. Really, she flounces. Then she stops. "And don't forget our yoga practice this afternoon." She resumes flouncing up the path.

"Do you have no screening mechanism at all?" I say.

"Well, definitely not like the state-of-the-art technology that you and Jennifer are working with. Honestly, I thought it was obvious that with Zoe gone you and Arlene are the main competitors. I mean, isn't that what everyone has been saying? Did I miss something?"

I groan.

"No, I'm serious. I was trying to get into the whole thing, even though I'm basically dead against competition. I thought it was very big of me."

I groan again.

"Quit it," Isabel snaps. "Are you and Arlene competing in that race at the end of the month?"

"Yes, we are," I say.

"Then what is the big deal? Does Arlene not know that she'll be participating? Are they going to blindfold her and push her into the water?"

"Isabel, do you not have any appreciation for nuance? For subtlety?"

Isabel gives me no helpful response.

"For psychological agenda? The mental game?" I prod.

"Oh, head games," Isabel says, leaning back, understanding on her face. "You were trying to outfox Arlene? Intimidate her? Throw her off balance?" Her face is split by a wide grin.

"What's so funny?"

"Maybe the next time you try to go one-on-one with a six-foot Amazonian athlete, you should wear cherry lip gloss instead of raspberry?"

I chew on my bottom lip to surreptitiously remove the last, lingering evidence of watermelon lip gloss. "That's nice."

"I think you're probably nice enough for both of us, don't you?" She shakes her head. "I need a smoke." She wanders into the woods.

Chapter Ten
Does a Bear Smoke in the Woods?

Most of my instincts tell me to go back to the cabin to the normal girls who don't blurt out every single thing that pops into their heads. This would be the sensible thing to do. But curiosity gets the better of me, not to mention the fact that it's an unusually dry July and Big Jack will have a mad cow if he catches Isabel smoking.

Isabel is sitting on a boulder puffing away by the time I catch up with her. A long stream of mauve-colored smoke curls up around her like a cashmere scarf.

"Smoking in the woods is like …" I stop and search for the right words. "Smoking in the woods." I decide to go for clarity. (God's most faithful angel, according to Mr. Hong.)

"Thanks for the tip," she says, taking another drag.

"Seriously, you could be sent home if Big Jack catches you."

"I'm still having trouble believing that I'm spending the summer in a place where people are called Big Jack."

I stand with my mouth half open. Attractive, I'm sure, but I don't know how to proceed. I wouldn't mind rewinding to her comment about how I liked Karim or her outrageous claim that she's never wrong or maybe her inappropriate comment to Arlene. Or, I could just continue with the whole smoking thing because, even now, she's butting her cigarette out on a tree that's as dry as kindling.

I decide that it's all too much, none of my business anyway. I turn to leave, at which point I walk into the wall of black-and-red checkered flannel that is Big Jack.

Big Jack with a smile on his face is like Santa Claus on Boxing Day — friendly, relaxed, kind of relieved.

Big Jack with no smile on his face is like one of Hell's Angels in the morning without coffee.

Big Jack with a scowl on his face, watching someone use one of his precious trees as an ashtray? You don't want to know.

"I can't believe we have to clean the boys' bathrooms, too," I say. "It's inhumane."

"Well, at least he didn't make us use our toothbrushes."

"I wasn't even smoking. It's so unfair." I pull on

the yellow rubber gloves and head into one of the stalls with a bucket and scrub brush. Almost immediately I'm out again, gasping. I close the door behind me. "I am going to be scarred for life."

"You're such a drama queen." Isabel rolls her eyes, pulls open the door and walks inside. Seconds later, those very eyes are two huge circles; they have seen more than they should. Isabel bolts.

I find her outside gulping fresh air like it's water and she's been lost in the desert for days.

"Who's the drama queen?"

"Who knew boys could be so nasty?"

"Hey!" A voice comes from above, and then a body plummets to the ground.

I look down. "Hey, Marcus." Marcus Tremblay has been falling out of trees for as long as I've known him. He wants to be a stuntman. If he lives.

"Are you okay?" Isabel looks down at the scrambled heap of Marcus and offers him a hand up.

Sheepishly, he shakes his head. "I'm okay. I must be, um, slipping."

I groan at the pun because I've known Marcus for eight years and am therefore obligated to groan. He was a geek then, and he is a geek now. But a likeable geek.

"Huh," says Isabel.

"This is Marcus. This is Isabel."

"Great hair," Marcus says, pulling up his pants, which have slipped, revealing boxer shorts covered in yellow parrots.

"Thanks. So, you just go around falling out of trees on purpose? Doesn't it hurt?"

"Not if you do it right. It's all about muscle relaxation and impact preparedness."

Isabel looks up at the tree, then down at the ground. "And that was?"

"Not my best work," he admits. "But I heard 'boys are nasty' and I lost my concentration."

I point to the bathroom. "Step inside stall number three and tell me if there's any other possible conclusion."

"Would it be fair to ask why you were in the boys' bathroom in the first place?"

"Hmm. Why don't you take that one, Isabel?"

Isabel shrugs. "Seems that the woods is a no-smoking area."

"Big Jack?"

"Big Jack."

Marcus looks at me. "You were smoking?" He sounds incredulous.

I shake my head. "No, but apparently I was an accessory," I say, remembering Big Jack's lengthy speech on the subject. "And in this town that's a hanging offense." A brilliant idea suddenly occurs to me. "Hey, there is a way that you could redeem your gender."

He looks at me with hopeful suspicion in his eyes. I've seen this look in his eyes before. It usually flicks on after we've had a conversation of more than twenty words. He has a little crush on me. Has had for eight years. Every summer he tells me we were meant to be together, and every summer I let him down easily.

"What?"

"You could volunteer to do the boys' bathroom for us. We're already late for our yoga class and it would really be, you know, swell, if you'd do that." I admit I put a little bit more emphasis into the "swell" than necessary, and I bite my lower lip just slightly at the same time. It could be construed as flirting.

"Kind of a damsel-rescuing thing?"

"Exactly."

He takes a deep bow and picks up the bucket. "It would be my pleasure."

As he walks into the washroom, I feel a small twinge of guilt.

"Thanks, Marcus. You're a prince," I call after him. I look at Isabel and give her a thumbs-up. "Let's go."

She picks up the other bucket, but doesn't follow me. I remember her inability to be hurried. "C'mon. We're already late."

"I'm going to stay here. Nice work setting the feminist movement back fifty years, though. Impressive."

Chapter Eleven
Downward-Facing Spiral

"Downward-facing dog," Shell says firmly in a monotone voice that is the yoga version of bossy.

We're in the gym with mats and baggy clothes — some of us with hidden licorice for sustenance. Our hands are on the ground in front of us, our butts are in the air as far as humanly possible and our feet are flat (but not quite because this is really tough) on the floor.

"You have very tight hamstrings," Shell observes in the same monotone as she wanders past. Then she puts her fingers in my belt loops and yanks my pelvis upward. "You should feel like you're being pulled skyward," she says. "Ever skyward. Always skyward. And don't forget to breathe."

I do take a deep breath — right before I crash down on my elbows. Others have done the same. Downward-facing dog is deceptively difficult. Shell makes it look easy. Her flexibility is astonishing considering that she is almost twenty years old. She folds and bends like she could slide inside an envelope.

"How about Dog-flattened-by-traffic?" I suggest as I plummet gracelessly to the floor once again.

Shell seems horrified at my joke and moves promptly into sun salutations, which are supposed to charge and cleanse the blood and shift the energy to a *chakra* I never knew I had.

"Breathe," she keeps saying, as if we'll forget.

Isabel joins us somewhere between the Tree pose and the Clam stretch. Jennifer gives me an I-told-you-so look, meaning, I assume, that she is right — this Isabel person will be a problem.

And then, just as I am collapsing from the weight of my upper body for the third time, I notice a set of familiar running shoes. I follow the shoe to calf to thigh to torso to head and long brown hair. A broken wing where an arm should be. It's Zoe! Zoe is here! I jump to my feet.

"How? What? Why? How?" I bombard her with questions as it sinks in that she isn't a hologram, a figment of my imagination. She's really here.

"Turns out that my arm wasn't as badly broken as they thought, although personally I just think I'm an excellent healer."

Trust Zoe to turn healing into a competitive event.

Shell officially ends the class, although no one is listening because everyone has gathered around Zoe, welcoming her and asking their own questions.

I'm pushed out of the way, but that's okay — the entire summer now stretches comfortably in front of me. Summer is saved.

Isabel is in the corner, still holding the Pose of the Child. She looks like she's really into it.

"Zoe's here," I say.

"I noticed." She gets up on her knees and then bends backward with the ease of an invertebrate.

"You're pretty good at this."

"I used to do it with my mother. She ran off with the yoga instructor, but I kept up the poses. It's bittersweet."

I look at the crown of her head and decide that it's impossible to read sincerity in the zig-zagged part of multi-colored hair.

"Huh?"

"I'm serious."

"I'm sorry," I manage to say.

"It's okay. She came back."

"That's good."

Isabel lifts her head and smiles. "Then she ran off with the plumber. For good. She's big at running away, my mom."

"Oh, Isabel." I don't quite know what to say. "That's sad."

"Yeah. Thanks." Her eyes meet mine. There's a shimmer of wetness in her eyes, and I don't doubt that she's telling the truth. In fact, in this moment, it hits me that Isabel will always tell the truth. I barely know her, but I know this. Then she moves into the Warrior pose. "Life's funny," she says. "So, you must be pretty happy to have your buddy here?"

"Yeah. Come meet her."

"Later."

I catch Zoe's glance and wave for her to join me outside. It's my turn. Once she's outside, I give her a big hug, and then we walk toward the sea. The air is spicier; the seagulls sound cheerful now instead of mournful. Everything about the day is more.

She takes a deep breath of the salty air. "I'm here."

"I'm so glad."

"I almost didn't come."

"Why not?"

"What can I do here? I can't compete in any of the events. They're putting me in the arts and crafts section! Me!"

Zoe and macaroni and glue guns and glitter is not a natural conclusion.

"I was hoping, well, actually I was sure they would make me an assistant swimming instructor."

I feel a little stab of something — guilt, maybe — as though I have betrayed her by being chosen to assist Karim. "Speaking of that, you know, swimming … I'm uh, um, the well, Karim, do you remember Karim? He's actually not very nice, actually. I'm assisting him."

"What are you babbling about?"

"I'm the assistant swimming coach. He wanted you, though." I am talking way too fast.

"Oh," she says.

"I'm sorry."

"Don't be. If it can't be me, I'm glad it's you."

"Really?"

"Of course." She gives me a little grimace. "At least I will be." She closes her eyes tightly. "There," she smiles. "I'm officially glad. Guess who came to see me at the hospital?"

"Brad Pitt?"

"He's busy or I'm sure he would have. Guess again."

"The prime minister?"

"Busy. Again?"

"Prince William?"

She's starting to look annoyed, but it's only mild Zoe annoyance, which means I have a ways to go. "Preparing to be king. Guess again."

"Mr. Clark?" He's a substitute teacher who had the worst breath in the history of worst breath: cigarettes, coffee and cheese. The Three Deadly C's.

"Eww, eww, eww. A-a-anna." She draws out the Anna as though she's close to meaning business.

"I give up."

"Corey."

"Corey-who-could or Corey-who-couldn't?"

She holds out her cast and I see the name scrawled in permanent ink, which is, in itself, quite promising. "Corey-who-couldn't," she says with pride.

"That is quite an accomplishment."

For clarification, there are two Coreys. Corey-who-could and Corey-who-couldn't. The names stem back to a birthday party. Both Coreys were invited, but only one came — obviously, Corey-who-could. It was Zoe's twelfth birthday and her first boy–girl event. She was devastated by Corey-who-couldn't's no-show and remained cold to him in a scorned-woman kind of way for years. I was never sure if it actually was scornage on his part or if he just couldn't come to the party. Anyway, that was the history of Corey-who-couldn't, who was now apparently Corey-who-did.

"He brought a big basket of stuff. Isn't that romantic?"

"What kind of stuff?" The reporter in me surfaces. "I need details." Zoe's love life was always more exciting than mine. It wasn't as though boys never asked me out, just not the really great guys. Zoe accused me of holding out for a prince; she said I only ever wanted the boy I couldn't get.

She shrugs her thin shoulders. Normally she was thin, but now she looked almost gaunt. I guessed the arm thing was responsible. "Just stuff."

I persist until she admits that the "stuff" consisted of two issues of *Sports Illustrated* and an enormous Toblerone bar that he had devoured almost half of during his visit.

"It's the thought that counts," she says.

I laugh. "Of course it is. It's actually pretty sweet."

"But not romantic?" she persists.

"I didn't say that."

"But you implied it."

"I did not. I just said it was sweet. Sweet is good."

"But it's not romantic."

I just groan.

"Anna, this is just like that time he gave me a compliment at the school dance and you laughed at him."

"He said your hair was the color of beer!"

"See!" Zoe pokes a slender finger at me. "You're doing it again."

I give in and announce that Corey-who-couldn't is romantic in a very masculine, testosterone-driven way. This makes Zoe happy, so I'm happy.

"What's the deal with this Isabel person?"

This Isabel person. Jennifer has obviously already updated Zoe on all the really important camp news. The girl is efficient. "What have you heard?"

"That she's a troublemaker. That she doesn't like swimming. That she doesn't fit in. That she needs a new hairdresser."

"That's quite a bit."

"So, is it true?"

"Well, she hasn't really caused any trouble yet." I pause, wondering whether to tell Zoe about the smoking debacle. But then I'd have to add the part about the bathroom cleaning and the business with Marcus and on and on and on. "She doesn't like swimming. Maybe she doesn't fit in. Her hair is inexplicable. You know Jennifer — she's a control freak."

"I guess." But Zoe doesn't sound convinced. She hasn't ever really gotten over being tossed out of Jennifer's inner circle. Sometimes I think she'd like back in.

"It's just so great that you're here!" I say again. "I thought the summer was doomed."

"Well, I'm here to save the day. It's so good to see you. I missed you so much."

For an instant, I feel a flash of guilt that I haven't really thought about her for the last few days. "Me, too."

When we get to the beach, we find our log, sit down and watch the tide. It's free time. Kids are running around, chasing each other with sea kelp whips and screaming into the wind.

"Can you even believe that we're in charge of them?"

"It's a little weird," she agrees and we giggle. For a while that's all we do, just sit there and giggle about nothing that's even remotely funny, and I'm perfectly happy.

When we get up to head back to camp, I notice Isabel walking along the edge of the forest. Her back is to us.

"Hey, Isabel," I call out.

Isabel turns and waits for us to catch up.

Zoe smiles her most winning smile and relief passes through me. I want Zoe to like Isabel. It will make things so, so, so much easier if she does.

Zoe holds out her left hand to shake, but it looks forced, affected. Isabel shakes it anyway.

"Zoe, this is Isabel. Isabel, this is Zoe." My voice sounds a little breathy, not quite me.

"How's your arm?" Isabel asks.

Zoe smiles bravely and shrugs. I recognize her wounded impression immediately. Usually she employs it with good-looking boys. "I'll survive," Zoe says.

Isabel says nothing and I realize I am holding my breath. This is all wrong. I can feel the tension in the air, and I know it's up to me.

"Isabel's assisting in fine arts this year. Maybe she can show you around," I say to Zoe. "Zoe's going to help out, too," I add, somewhat unnecessarily.

A wan smile crosses Zoe's face. "I've been coming here for years, Anna. I think I know my way around." She says this cheerfully, but I can hear the put-down. So does Isabel, I'm sure, but her face registers nothing.

"If you change your mind, let me know," Isabel says. "We're doing watercolors now. The kids are pretty excited about it. A couple of them are even doing portraits of Karim and Anna down at the pool." She smiles.

I grin at this for no reason except that Isabel is being friendly and not one bit sarcastic. And maybe because someone, somewhere, is painting my picture.

"I hear that water's not your favorite subject," says Zoe. The change of subject is awkward, even though she's still smiling cheerily.

Isabel's smile disappears. "I'm okay with watercolors."

Zoe actually looks a little embarrassed, which she should, but she keeps the phony smile on her face.

"I'm going to have a shower," Isabel says. She takes a fork in the path and heads back to the cabin. I resist the urge to tell her that it's almost dinnertime and could she please not be late.

"What was that about?" I ask Zoe, once Isabel is out of earshot.

Zoe's eyes expand, becoming large and innocent. "What?"

"Do not baby-deer-eyes me," I say.

"I don't know. It's just that everything's so ... different. My arm and all these new people, and then along comes Rainbow-girl offering to show me around. It's just too much."

"She was just trying to be helpful and friendly. Trust me, it doesn't exactly come easy to her."

"What, being friendly to me is such a chore?"

I forgot that Zoe takes everything personally. How could I have forgotten this?

"Just friendly in general. She's just, I don't know, blunt, I guess. And really honest. So for her to be friendly —"

"To me."

"Well, that dig about the water? That was a nice thing for you to say?"

"We can't all be as nice as you, Anna, Queen of Nice."

Zoe's put-downs are never particularly clever, but they are sharp and to the point.

I can't believe Zoe and I are fighting so soon after she has arrived, so I do the only thing I can. "I'm sorry," I say. The words feel forced, but I can see their immediate effect.

"It's okay."

"I just want you to like Isabel."

"Why? Why is this Isabel person important? Why isn't it enough that you and I are together again? I thought you'd be happy."

"I am happy," I say. "Of course I am."

It suddenly occurs to me that Zoe is jealous, but this hardly seems possible. We're never jealous of each other. It's not what we do. Even when Zoe beats me at everything — that's just the way it is, the natural order. It's pretty simple.

Hesitantly I try out this new theory. "You're not jealous of Isabel, are you?"

She shakes her head back and forth like this may be the most ridiculous thing she's ever heard. "Of course not," she says softly, and I feel stupid for even mentioning it. "I'm just being a baby. I expected things to be the same and of course they aren't." She lifts her cast. "Maybe I shouldn't have come."

"Don't say that." I put my arm around her shoulders. "We're going to have as much fun as ever. We're together. That's enough, isn't it?"

Zoe doesn't answer.

Chapter Twelve
Bad Teenage Role Model Takes Two Tumbles

Waking up the next morning is like waking up on the set of a science-fiction movie. Things are more or less the same and, with Zoe here, even the way they should be. Yet everything feels different. And it's not just because of the uneasy air between Zoe and Isabel.

And then Mr. Hong is in the room, ranting about the truth. "You have to search for it, be relentless. And then you write it so that it grabs a person by the throat and throws them to the floor."

The first time he said this I told him it sounded a little violent. I was going for funny, but he lit up. "Exactly! There is an element of violence in speaking the truth!"

I shake my head to get rid of the memory and get out of bed. I stretch vigorously and try out one of Shell's yoga poses. Zoe is here and it's what I wanted the most, so it's bad form — and maybe even bad luck — to question a dream coming true. Isn't it?

"You shouldn't begin with such a strenuous pose," Shell mumbles, still half-asleep. "Try a sun salutation first. Greet the dawn with a ..." then her voice fades back to sleep before she can complete the saying.

I do a bunch of awkward sun salutations and, before I know it, Mags and Gin and Jennifer are beside their bunks doing the same thing: the Bridge, the Warrior, the Sideways-facing Dog (too early for the Downward-facing). Then Shell is up, scampering back and forth, looking decidedly ruffled and untranquil as she tries to bring some sort of order to this impromptu yoga fest.

Finally everyone is on the floor except Zoe and Isabel. Shell beams at us as we hold the Plow position.

We finish off with some quiet stretches, ending up cross-legged in the Lotus position.

Shell presses her hands in front of her and bows slightly. "Namaste," she says. We return the greeting.

Yesterday she told us that this meant "the spirit in me greets the spirit in you." I like that. It's like, who I really am says hi to who you really are. It occurs to me that this is what is missing — the feeling that I really, truly know who anyone in this room is.

"Awesome leadership," Shell says to me as we stand up.

I'm a little surprised to hear this, and my automatic response is to check Zoe's reaction. But it seems that Zoe is still sleeping. Isabel, however, looks at me with a half-smile on her face. She gives me a sideways thumbs-up before slumping back into her pillow. "You are way too energetic this morning," she groans.

"The better to encourage my prize pupil to swim a width of the pool today," I say in a very sinister voice, heading over to her bunk. I notice a glass only a quarter full of water beside her bed. I pick it up and hold it over her head.

"Perhaps we'll try it one drop at a time," I threaten.

Gin calls out encouragement and Charmaine screams because she is a screamer. Shell looks officially concerned, but mostly amused.

"You wouldn't dare," Isabel looks up at me, unblinking, challenging.

"Oh, wouldn't I?" I tilt the glass and watch the stream of liquid climb down the side toward Isabel's face.

But then I hear Zoe moan behind me. Her cast looks awkward as she tries to get into a sitting position.

"Can you help me?" she asks.

I put down the glass of water and go to the side of her bunk.

"I don't think the top bunk is a very good idea," I say, repeating what I said the night before.

"But I always sleep up here," Zoe had said, and she says this again now. "I just need some help getting down," she adds tersely.

I help her navigate the ladder and then carry her stuff to the bathroom. At the door she whispers, "I'm sorry. I just hate ..." She waves her cast at me. "I just hate this."

After breakfast and getting Zoe settled at the Fine Arts building, which is at the opposite end of the campground from the pool, I race over to avoid a grimace from the Great Disapprover, Karim. As I enter the change room, I rip off my sweats and fly past Isabel.

"Hey," she calls out.

"Can't talk," I say. "Later."

At the entrance to the pool, I slow down and attempt to skid to a halt, but because it is a pool deck and there is water, I keep on skidding. I don't actually halt until I am on my butt in front of a group of surprised-looking children. Not my most dignified entrance.

One girl looks like she is ready to cry. The others are laughing gleefully. Filled with glee. Absolutely brimming.

"Are you okay? Did you hurt yourself?" asks the almost-crying girl. Her name is Beverley, I think.

"Yeah, yeah, just my pride," I say, wondering if I've broken anything important.

Then Karim is there, holding out his hand, which I take because I am feeling a little woozy from the fall.

Before I can say thank you, he says, "You're late."

My gratitude melds into a desire to slap him across the face like they do in the movies or, at the very least, throw a martini at him. He adds, "Are you okay?" but it's too late. The slap is still fresh in my mind and it gives me more satisfaction than his concern, which seems insincere at best.

"I'm okay," I mutter. "It's just so slippery."

"And that's why we … what, kids?" He turns and addresses the throng behind him like he is the mayor of Whoville.

"Never run on the pool deck," they scream out.

Karim tips his glasses forward so that I can see his dark eyes. They appear to be twinkling, even though there is not a trace of a smile on his face. "That's right," he nods. "You got that, Anna Banana?"

I manage a smile for the benefit of the kids, but when he turns, I can't help it. I stick my tongue out at him.

Bad move, I know. Bad, bad teenage role model. But the kids love it and hoot with laughter. Isabel, who has seen the whole thing, shakes her head like she can't believe it.

Karim turns slowly, like a sheriff who has heard the click of a revolver.

Little Beverley, little loudmouth Beverley, screams, "Anna Banana stuck her tongue out at you. Very far," she adds, as if this is crucial information.

I feel myself turn red, but I smile as though I don't know what this poor, demented child is babbling about. Unfortunately the rest of the kids chant their corroboration and I realize I am hopelessly outnumbered, as well as completely guilty.

I do the only thing I can. I shrug.

"You're not even denying it?" he asks.

"I may have had an involuntary tongue-muscle reflex due to my, er, accident," I offer. Not bad.

Then I realize that Karim is still moving forward and, before I know it, he picks me up in the manner of a caveman and flings me over his shoulder like I am a piece of venison or whatever it was that cavemen hunted — woolly mammoth, perhaps — and carts me down to the deep end of the pool where one does not have to be a rocket scientist to figure out what he's planning to do.

The kids follow behind like a pack of joyful hyenas. I could try to fight, but I'd end up flapping my fists against his back, which would add to the ridiculousness of the scene, not to mention be a cliché of a damsel in distress. And then the whole damsel-being-carried-away-to-the-tower motif doesn't seem like such a terrible image to me. Plus being carried so easily by Karim is not completely horrible. My face is burning with embarrassment, so that when he asks the horde whether or not he should throw me into the water, I find myself casting a silent vote for him to heave me in.

And heave me he does. As I hit the cool water, I let myself sink like a pebble to the bottom of the pool. I look up and see a blurry montage of laughing faces. Their giggles travel down to me, muffled by the curtain of water between us. The distortion of their faces is interesting, but I'm running out of air. I swim underwater to the shallow end of the pool and emerge, making a big show of stretching. "That was very refreshing," I say.

Even Karim is laughing now, and all of my earlier spite and vengeance shrivels away to a little curd of nothing. All I can think is *Cute, he's so cute.*

I disgust myself.

The rest of the morning goes smoothly. Karim returns to being the professional and I do my best to regain my composure. It helps that the kids are oblivious to anything other than learning to swim and splashing each other in the face. It's exhausting, but fun. I'm careful to make sure that no one drowns.

Isabel makes some progress, but there's always a look of fear just below the surface. Karim is good with her, I have to admit. He has a way of getting her to go a little further each time but never beyond her comfort level. Today he has her actually dipping her face in the water as she practices the front crawl and, even though her movements are jerky, she manages to get across the width of the pool.

"Hurray!" I shout out. "Good for you."

The other kids, who have taken Isabel on as a kind of oversized mascot, shout out, "Yay, Is." That's her nickname — Is — nothing embarrassing about it.

Isabel waves back as though she has just completed a marathon. She looks a little embarrassed, but pleased as well. The whole thing makes me feel warm inside.

I have to hand it to Isabel. You can see how difficult this is for her. It's in the way her body tenses up just before she approaches the water. She goes from calm, cool and collected to tense, taut and terrified. By the time her body is in the water, she is one hundred percent focused on the task at hand. I can tell she isn't even conscious of Karim's hands on her shoulders as he gives her some instruction or advice, standing close enough so that she must be able to smell that dizzying combination of coconut suncreen, chlorine and him.

"Um, Miss Banana," Beverley tugs at my bathing suit strap from the deck of the pool. "My shampoo fell and it's dripping all over the floor. People could slip. People could die!" Her eyes are wide with alarm.

"Or we could all go up in bubbles."

"Miss Banana, this is serious."

"Bev, Bev," I say as I crawl out of the pool. "I'm just joking."

"And it's my best shampoo. I got it from Santa."

"Oh. Well, what are we waiting for? This is serious." And then, because of my earlier deck-slipping mishap, I do an exaggerated speed-walk to the change room that makes Beverley giggle and pronounce that my bum looks funny when I do that.

I reach the Santa shampoo, which is, as it turns out, packaged to look like Santa himself, complete with protruding belly. It is this very belly that has stopped the bottle from emptying most of its contents. I hose down the floor until every lethal bubble has slipped down the drain.

"Here you go, kiddo." I hand the bottle to her. "Next time put the top on before you put it down." I feel very grown-up and responsible — almost super-heroish. I like this role, I decide. I look around to see if there are other small children I might save.

I leave Beverley (not Bev, as she politely informs me) shampooing happily (twice, because that's what the bottle suggests). As I leave, I add a mental note to my list of things to do this summer: help Beverley loosen up.

When I return to the pool area, Isabel is sitting on the edge of the pool, chatting — unrobotically now — to Karim. Zoe is over at the bleachers. She waves her good arm at me.

"Hey." I sit down beside her. "Who's sticking the glitter on the macaroni back at fine arts?"

"I just finished. And trust me, there is no fine art involved. There are going to be a lot of parents looking for a place to stash an ugly ashtray."

"So, no budding Martha Stewarts?"

Zoe grimaces. "I can barely stand it, not being outside, not being near the water. I begged them to give me a waterproof cast, but they said it was too soon."

I murmur sympathetically. I can't imagine being this close to water and not being able to go in. "Maybe you could hold your arm over your head and just go in up to your waist?"

Zoe gives me such a look of disbelief that we both burst out laughing. "That is the worst idea I've ever heard," she says.

"I know. I'm sorry. I just want you to have fun this summer. Will it be okay?"

"Anna, get serious. It's paste and glitter and finger-paints. I'll be lucky if I don't die from fume inhalation."

"I'm sorry," I say again.

"Nah," she says, lifting her good hand. "I have an idea that will save the summer." She pauses for dramatic effect. Her eyebrow is raised. She is waiting.

"And the idea is ...?"

"Jennifer reminded me that, with me out of the picture, it's up to you to win the swimming race. So —"

"Do we care what Jennifer thinks?" I interrupt.

"Well." She looks uncomfortable. "Not ordinarily, but even Napoleon had a few good ideas."

"I thought this was your idea."

"Do you even know what the idea is?"

"No ..."

"That would be because you keep interrupting me!"

"Speak."

"Thank you." She pauses dramatically. "I am going to train you to beat Arlene."

"Oh my," I say. I let the words sit in the air, propped up in a bubble by her happy mood. But the bubble has to be burst eventually and better sooner than later. "That's not possible," I say. "We both know it. I mean, that's not what I'm saying to everyone else, especially

Jennifer, because, well, because. But seriously, Zoe. We both know how this is going to turn out."

"I know nothing of the kind. Under my tute ... what's that word?"

"Tutelage," I supply grimly.

"Yes, that's the one. Under my expert tutelage, we can't lose."

I don't remind her that even she has only ever beat Arlene that one time, under suspect circumstances. And I never beat Zoe. But she has said we.

It should give me hope.

It does not.

Chapter Thirteen
Being Liked: Mandatory

"Those two look pretty cozy over there," Zoe says, glancing in the direction of Karim and Isabel.

I'm still mulling over what it will mean to be a project of Zoe's. This isn't really something that's come up before because, mostly, Zoe's projects involve Zoe. But she always takes things on with maximum intensity; there's no reason to think this will be any different.

"Listen, Zoe. This idea —"

"Sh-pt," she whispers. "They're coming over."

I look up. Sure enough, Isabel and Karim are headed our way.

"Hi, Zoe. I heard you were back," Karim says. "I thought it would take more than a broken arm to keep you away."

Karim's voice is open and friendly. Apart from the glee on his face moments after he threw me in the pool, I have yet to be on the receiving end of such friendliness. The injustice is really ticking me off.

Zoe giggles happily and says something about how he needs to sign her cast. She hands him a pen.

Isabel sits beside me.

"Good job today," I whisper. "Really great."

"I'm just trying to be the best darn Bottom-feeder there ever was."

"Now don't get too proud," I say, and we chuckle. It's not really a laugh, and it's definitely not a giggle — it's just a chuckle, but Zoe's head twists toward us.

"What's so funny?"

We shrug at the same time.

"I was just telling Karim about our plan," Zoe continues.

This completely wipes off any smile I might have had on my face. Two seconds ago it was an idea, one that she sh-pted in the interest of secrecy. Now it's a public plan? "We don't really have a plan-plan," I say to Zoe. "There would be no point, remember?"

"Oh, Anna. You're too modest." She looks up at Karim. "She almost beat me last month at a swim meet."

"I did not. I was at least four strokes behind." It's true. At least four. I counted.

"And she's going to beat Arlene Breckner this year. I'm going to make sure."

"I believe it," Isabel says.

"How about it, Karim? Will you help out?" Zoe asks.

I flinch as though someone has pulled the hairs on the back of my neck. What is she doing involving Karim?

"I don't know about that," he says. "I think I have to stay neutral."

"No, you don't," Zoe says.

Karim is clearly uncomfortable.

"Karim doesn't think I can do it." I say this out loud, which comes as a shock to me. But once the words are out there, I can't do anything about it except sit a little taller. Trust me. If I could take them back, I would.

"I didn't say that."

"I didn't say you said it. I said it's what you were thinking. Thinking, saying — two different things." Who is saying these stupid things and why won't she shut up?

"So now you're a mind reader?" he asks.

"It's not that tough a read."

I can actually sense Isabel's smile, although I don't dare to look at her. I see Zoe's frown.

"Um, hello," Zoe interjects. "I'm sure Karim thinks it's a good idea, don't you?"

Karim doesn't even look at Zoe. He's too busy looking at me in a way that, despite my earlier pronouncement, I can't read. It's starting to make me uncomfortable, but I refuse to look away first on principle.

"Ahem," Isabel says, quite clearly, but for no particular reason as she doesn't say anything further.

"I believe in competition," Karim says. "But as the lifeguard, I can't show favoritism."

"But you don't think I can win," I say. Why am I still doing this? It's as though my vocal cords have a mind of their own and they are a beat ahead of my brain, which is screaming, Shut up!

Karim smiles. "God, you are a bulldog. Okay, I'll tell you what I think. If you cared half as much about winning a race as you do about winning an argument, Arlene Breckner wouldn't stand a chance. You could swim circles around her. But I don't think you will."

And with this frustrating and, face it, enigmatic statement, he turns and walks to the far end of the pool.

"That was a little weird," Zoe says, putting things nicely in perspective as we leave the pool area. "What's his problem?"

"I don't really think he has a problem," I say. "I mean, clearly he hates me, but it doesn't seem to be a problem for him."

"He doesn't hate you," Isabel says quickly.

"Why? Did he say something?" Zoe jumps on Isabel's comment like a mongrel on leftovers.

Silently, I will Isabel not to add her noodle-brained theory that I like Karim. For one thing, it's not true, but I also don't want Zoe to hear this. I don't know why; I just don't.

"Why would he hate her?" Isabel says, to my relief.

"I wasn't the one who said it." Zoe sounds defensive.

"Okay, okay," I interrupt. "Maybe hate is too strong, although I'm not convinced. Anyway, who cares what he thinks?"

"Did you do something last year to piss him off?" asks Zoe, obviously not quite up to speed on the whole "who cares what he thinks" concept.

"No," I say. "I barely had anything to do with him. I don't even know very much about him except that he's a competitive swimmer. He always wins the Counselor Race."

"*Was* a competitive swimmer. He wrecked his shoulder this spring. He had surgery, but it doesn't look like he'll get his speed back," Isabel says.

Both Zoe and I look at her. We've been coming here for years and years. Why does she know this and we don't?

"He told the class this morning. Somebody asked about the scar," Isabel explains. "That was before your heroic entrance."

"What heroic entrance?" Zoe asks.

"Oh, nothing," I say dismissively. I'm still back with Karim's shoulder. I hadn't even noticed a scar.

"What heroic entrance?" Zoe persists.

"I slipped on the pool deck. It was no big deal. Listen, I really don't like this whole training idea. I mean, I don't mind racing Arlene, but let's just let what happens … happen, okay? I don't want to turn my whole summer into a competition."

"You're exaggerating. It would be, like, an hour a day. And do you think she's not training? Arlene is at it every chance she gets!"

"I know, I know. Probably with two of the smaller campers strapped to her legs for weights. She probably has lead woven into her braids to make her heavier — possibly ingests little ball bearings with her morning oatmeal ..."

Zoe sighs. "C'mon, Anna. It'll be fun. No pressure. Who cares who wins?"

Isabel gives me a funny look and then says she's off to her shift at the Fine Arts building.

"See you later," I call.

"When should we start?" Zoe asks with such enthusiasm that I know I can't say no to her.

It will give her something to do, which will make her happy and useful-feeling. And that will make me happy and useful-feeling. Besides, the race isn't going to go away so I might as well be prepared for it, although this will not change the outcome one piddly little iota.

"How about after lunch?" I say.

Zoe squeals and then squeezes me with her good arm. "You won't regret this," she says. "I feel just like Dr. Jekyll." She chuckles happily.

I wonder about this comment for a moment or two and decide that Zoe's reading tastes make it likely that she has no idea she's just made me her monster protégée/alter ego.

"I'll meet you at the cafeteria, okay? I forgot something at the pool."

"I'll wait," says Zoe.

"It's okay. I'll meet you there."

Zoe looks uncertain, but she walks off. I feel a pull of guilt, but I need to talk to Karim. I walk back to the pool area, where he's checking the chlorine levels. I see it — the neat, white scar on the back of his shoulder. It looks too small to have been part of something that's done so much damage.

He doesn't notice me until I'm beside him. "I just wanted to make sure we were done here," I say.

Karim looks around at the deserted pool deck. "Everyone's gone. What would you do?"

"I, um. Yeah, right. Okay, I'll just go."

Karim nods and heads over to the supply shed. I know I should just leave. In fact, every single part of my body agrees with this, except for my feet. I look down at them, nicely trimmed with pink nail polish, but they're not moving. And then they are, toward the shed.

Most of Karim is inside the building.

"I'm sorry," I say.

"What are you sorry about?" He sounds gruff and tired. His hand reaches across his broad, smooth chest to massage his shoulder. I don't even think he knows what he's doing.

"I just heard about your injury."

His hand immediately comes down to his side. He looks angry.

"I just heard that you can't race anymore." I don't

even know why I'm still talking — every tense molecule in the air between us is warning me to stop.

Karim says nothing. He turns back into the shed and grabs a bottle of chlorine. He moves over to the pool and dumps some of it into the water. "Fine. Thanks."

I get as far as the exit. "You really don't like me, do you?"

Karim puts the lid back on the bottle. His shoulders droop. "Does it matter if I like you?"

"Aha! You don't like me."

"I didn't say that."

"You didn't say that you didn't not like me."

He looks a little confused.

"You're a counselor! You have to like me."

"Does everybody have to like you, Anna?"

What an incredibly stupid question. All I can do is gawk. He shrugs and goes back to his work. Apparently, I've been dismissed. I leave, but his question follows me. *Yes*, I think. *Yes, they do.* This is pretty much the one thing that I know for sure.

"We haven't even talked about 'mentionables' yet," Zoe says, as we make our way down to the beach after lunch. "Any cute CITs? The guy over at rock climbing looked like a possibility. I think his name is Jake. Jennifer said he's new."

"What about Corey-who-Couldn't?" I tease.

"He might come to see me on Visitor's Day!"

"That's only a week from now," I say. "I can't believe how fast this month is going."

"Back to guys," Zoe says, like a boomerang. "Who do you have your eye on?"

"My eye?"

"Your eye, your heart, your head … any other body part you might think of."

"Who says I have my eye on anyone?" I ask, trying out righteous indignation, wondering if it will wash.

But Zoe only laughs. "Right. C'mon, spill. Who's the lucky object of your fantasy who will never become a reality?"

A disturbing thing happens. As soon as she asked the question, Karim comes into my head. But that isn't disturbing. Maybe it's weird because Karim hates me, but the disturbing thing is that for the first time in my life I want to hold something back from Zoe, keep something for myself. It's unprecedented.

"C'mon. You're thinking about somebody. I can see it right behind your eyes. Rock-climbing Jake?"

"I'm thinking about your crazy plan to coach me," I say. I tell myself that this isn't so much a lie as it is an improvisation. (Mr. Hong has trouble seeing the difference between the two.)

"It'll give me something to do," she says, as we reach the crest of the hill. "I just have to do something, you know? I'm going crazy here."

I look at her arm, rigid and useless when it should be crashing through waves. "Damned rooster."

"Damned rooster," she agrees.

We walk down the side of the hill toward the water, but the sand is uneven and Zoe slips before I can grab her. "Are you okay?"

She has tears in her eyes, but she gets up without taking my outstretched hand. "I hate this, Anna. I just hate this."

Chapter Fourteen
Invisible Lifeboat of Truth Sets Sail

Jennifer, Benita and Charmaine are at the beach when we arrive. They're watching something in the ocean and I wonder if it's a trapped killer whale. On closer scrutiny, I see it's Arlene.

"She's been out there for hours. I don't think she even stops for lunch," says Charmaine.

"Yes, she did," Benita says. "She had the salad bar."

"Low carb," Jennifer adds.

"No pressure," I mutter, as I push my kangaroo jacket over my head. For a minute I'm muffled in safe, warm, downy cotton and I can't see the intrepid Arlene pulling her way through the ocean like a greased-up seal.

Zoe says, "What?"

I say I didn't say anything.

"It's okay, Anna," she adds consolingly, proving that she heard me after all. "She'll wear out soon."

"I don't know about that," Charmaine says.

I see Zoe shoot a laser look at her, and Charmaine quickly adds, "But she's no match for you."

This is such an absurd comment that we all have to laugh.

For a minute or two we watch the dip and pull of Arlene's behemoth arms as though we're in a trance.

Zoe finally steers me toward the wharf. When we get there, Arlene is pulling herself up onto the ladder. Water runs off her bronzed self in rivulets. As she shakes the water out of her face, she sees us. "Zoe! I heard you were here," she says, friendly enough. For arch rivals, they've always been very civil to each other, at least face-to-face, that is. "Sorry about your arm."

"Yeah, well, what are you gonna do? Stupid accident."

"Yeah, I heard it was in the line of duty."

"Huh?" Zoe looks confused and turns to me. I suddenly realize that I haven't told her about the kitten-rescue version of her mishap.

"She means how you were trying to rescue the kitten stranded up on the barn roof," I fill in these missing details with a subtle arch of my brow.

Zoe pauses for only a millisecond. "Oh, right," she nods. "Yeah, it's fine."

Arlene narrows her eyes while she wrings seawater out of her hair. "Well, for future notice, nine out of ten times, a cat will find its way down on its own." Then she picks up her tote bag and heads off to the shore. Over her shoulder she calls out, to me presumably, "Good luck."

When she is out of earshot, Zoe gives me a withering look. "Kitten rescuing? That's the best you could come up with?"

"It sounded better at the time. It's all in the delivery."

Zoe looks unconvinced.

"I should have stuck with the you-wanted-to-beat-the-rooster angle?"

Zoe has the grace to giggle at this. "It was a drama exercise," she says, as she pulls a whistle out of her pocket.

"What's that?" I ask stupidly.

"Coach Zoe, at your service."

"Oh, brother," I mutter. "That is a dangerous combination." I don't have a chance to explain why this is so dangerous because Zoe blasts away and orders me into the drink.

I salute and say something about "Captain Bligh," but she doesn't hear me. She's too busy blasting away on her whistle and yelling instructions. "Straighten those legs. Pull. Faster. Faster." I have to stop swimming just to hear her.

"Don't look back," she yells.

"There's nobody following me," I yell back.

"There's always somebody following you," she screams. But she looks really pleased with herself.

I submerge again and try to drown out the noise. When I haul myself out of the water an hour later, I am exhausted. Zoe looks perky and exhilarated and well rested. "I think I'm really cut out for this coaching gig," she says.

I look at her happy face, my breath coming in big, urgent gasps. I lie flat on my back on the wharf and it feels like everything — trees, wharf, water — is circling around me. In this spinning state, it occurs to me that coaching and bossing someone around are very similar.

"Don't you think?" Zoe persists. "This may be my calling."

I manage to get out, "It ... might ... be."

I hear voices coming from the water — voices and giggling — but I'm too dizzy to look up. Then I hear something thump against the side of the wharf. I get up on my elbows. It's Rock-climbing Jake and Skater-dude, whose name I don't know. Jennifer is in the middle of the canoe. With a bit of black eyeliner and a wig, she'd be a dead ringer for Cleopatra.

"Come canoeing," they all say in one voice.

I say I'm too tired, but tell Zoe to go. She tries to convince me to go along. I convince her that five in a canoe is a catastrophe waiting to happen. She rolls her eyes, and they float away in a burst of giggles and conversation.

As my breath returns to normal, I give myself over to the pleasant sensation of the rocking waves and the scent of sun-soaked creosote and salt water. I open an eye lazily and watch a jet flume dissipate in the sapphire sky. Then I'm in a shadow. I hold my hand up to my face and raise my head to see who has dared to block my light and my perfect moment.

"You're going to have to do better than that if you want to beat Arlene."

It's Karim, and he's looking down at me, so I sit up immediately. He plunks himself beside me on the wharf with his feet dangling in the water. He's close enough that I can feel the heat of his body, but not so close that it makes sense for me to move.

"Who says I want to beat Arlene Breckner?" I say.

Karim laughs and shakes his head. "I thought you did."

Okay, okay. Training for a race without wanting to win, especially when I've yelled at him only this morning for not thinking I could do it, could be construed as a little, er, dim. But I will not let him win this one.

"I just meant that I'm more interested in doing my best," I say, with my back incredibly straight. "Of course I'd like to win, but I think it's more important to compete against one's own self." I say this with my nose slightly in the air as if it will give my words more lift, more prominence, more weight. But in my head, the words come ringing back to me: "against one's own self." Did I really say that? Mr. Hong would be in a frenzy.

Karim smiles even more. Damn those white teeth. "It's not personal, Anna. That's the thing you have to remember."

"Then why do people race?" A loophole — I'm looking for a loophole here.

He makes a sound like air escaping from a tire. "It's just …" He shakes his head. "It's like you need the other person — you need each other — to find out what you're made of, what you can really do."

He says this so sadly that it throws me off. "Hey," I say. "Aren't you supposed to be Mr. Impartial? Mr. Objective? Shouldn't you be keeping your opinions to yourself?"

"I'd give Arlene the same advice," he says.

"That's not true," I say, quite loudly, as though I'm a lawyer and have woken up in the middle of a trial with a really good objection. Hmm, I probably would be a very good lawyer. Quite persuasive. Maybe even a judge.

"What's not true?" Karim prods.

Where was I? Objecting — but to what? Then I remember. "As far as you're concerned, Arlene could swim blindfolded with one arm tied behind her back and still win."

Karim pulls one leg out of the water and swivels to face me.

"If Arlene were here, I would tell her that if you decided to show up — I mean, really show up — she would have to swim the best race of her life to beat you. That's what racing does."

Then he stands up. He isn't smiling anymore. I scramble up so as not to have the sitting-down disadvantage. "Anyway," he continues, "the reason I came down here was just to tell you that you were good with Beverley today. She's kind of intense and, well, I just thought you should know that you did a good job."

"Thanks," I say, flustered.

Karim looks as though he wants to say something more. But then he pulls his baseball cap low over his eyes, takes another quick look at the ocean and walks off.

Broad shoulders, narrow waist, lean, strong legs. Perfect posture. Swimming was what he was made for. A couple of counselors call out to him to come over. He raises a hand, but keeps walking. Come to think of it, he's almost always alone except when he's with little kids.

I shake these thoughts away. A mystery to add to the enigma of Karim is the last thing I need.

As I walk back to the cabin through the woods, I hear a snuffle through the underbrush. I push my way through. There on the other side sits Beverley, crying in a trying-not-to-cry kind of way.

"Bev ..." I begin. "... erley," I finish, because even in her grief she has shot me a look of correction. "What's up?" I sit beside her on a log.

"I want to go hoooome," she wails. She flings herself into my arms, practically sending me sprawling off my precarious perch.

"How come?"

"Nobody likes me. Everybody hates me," she says.

I'm very tempted to add the words, "Guess I'll go eat some worms" because that's how the song goes, but CIT training prevails.

"I'm sure that's not true," I say, doing an amazing impression of my mother that I instantly regret. "I don't hate you," I add.

"You have to not hate me," she blubbers with amazing accuracy.

Beverley keeps sobbing until my front is soaked. I sneak a look at my watch and realize that I am about to be late for a Cabin Seven powwow called by Jennifer.

"Okay, kiddo." I peel the sodden girl off my chest like an old Band-Aid. "Let's look at the facts. Do you have any evidence that supports your theory?" I am back to being a reporter, perhaps with a swig of Sherlock Holmes thrown in.

The tears suddenly dry up like a waterfall that has been dammed. "Shelby and Haley and Lucy all say that I can't be in charge of the Talent Show skit."

I swear, apart from the dirt streaks on her face, you'd never know she was crying only moments before. Her eyes are shining — glowing, actually — with fervor.

"I have the best ideas. Their ideas are all stupid. I should be in charge."

I look at the little girl in front of me and I have a Zoe flashback to sixth grade. It had to be a production of *Les Misérables* or nothing. The teacher refused, saying it was too ambitious. Let's just say it was lucky for Zoe that Ms. Gamble never found out who put the guinea pig turds in her desk later that week.

"Did you tell them that their ideas are stupid?" I ask. This is very probing and insightful stuff, I think. I may want to consider psychotherapy as well as all my other career opportunities. I'm busy picturing myself lecturing to a room full of renowned psychiatrists when I hear Beverley's voice. Oops. First rule of a good shrink is probably to pay attention to the whining.

"… so I said, 'Charlie Brown? That is so yuck.'"

"You said 'so yuck'?" I respond. "I'm kind of partial to Snoopy myself."

Beverley favors me with a completely dismissive look. It's another Zoe moment.

"So, what was your idea?"

"Well," she leans forward and then squirms a little with the excitement of it all. She gives it a dramatic pause. "*King Lear*."

"Bev … erley," I say. "Last year Cabin Two won for the Spit Skit. Are you familiar with it?" Every member of the cabin brushes his or her teeth and then spits into a cup, the contents of which the final brave soldier (the kind who eats bugs for a quarter) drinks. It's a real crowd-pleaser.

"Yes," she says, but with a note of absolute displeasure. Her arms are crossed tightly at her chest; her little foot taps the ground impatiently. "It's totally disgusting."

"Well, everyone else thought it was a winner. Don't you think you might be overestimating your audience just a little?"

"So I have to be disgusting to win the talent contest? I have to drink somebody else's spit?"

I shake my head that this is not what I meant. I try to imagine Shell reworking this little piece of advice into a life-affirming saying.

"Why are you smiling?" Beverley barks. "You're not taking me seriously." Her little nose seems slightly more pointed and her lips are pressed together. She looks as though she is ready to blow — not a battle I want or need right now. I decide this is a job for Beverley's counselor. I put my arm around her shoulders.

"Why don't we see what your counselor has to say about this?"

"My counselor is stupid."

As we make our way back to Beverley's cabin, she lists the ways in which she is misunderstood and why she should be cabin leader and why they should stage *King Lear* and why she should play Cordelia, the voice of reason, and why and why and why.

I listen to roughly one-third of her conversation before I strike psychotherapist off of my list of things to be. When we arrive at her cabin, I give her counselor (Sunny, it turns out) a brief overview. She responds with such a drawn-out sigh that I think a more appropriate name might have been Eeyore. Beverley shoots me a this-is-what-I-have-to-deal-with look.

"I'll see you at the pool tomorrow, okay, Beverley?"

Sunny/Eeyore waits until Beverley has gone inside before she whispers, "They're starting to call her 'Beverley Hills,' you know? Because of the attitude. It's not good."

When I walk inside my own cabin minutes later, the atmosphere is sizzling. Isabel and Zoe are facing each other like they're about to draw pistols. Shell is standing between them and she's speaking, turning her head from one to the other with almost rhythmic timing. I slink in without making a noise.

"... and the thing is," Shell is saying, "these are the defining moments, you know? You have to make a choice ... Do I take a chance and grab hold of the lifeboat of truth, or do I stay with the ship of easiness, even though it's sinking, because it's big and familiar and possibly has a satellite dish?"

I'm confused because I'm walking into this thing in the middle, but even Isabel and Zoe, who I assume have been here since Shell started talking, seem confused. And then Shell joins in with a frown, and soon we're all just standing around — a big old group of bewilderment.

"What's up?" I say brightly because somebody needs to say something.

Shell scratches her head. "I, um ..."

Isabel brushes past me. "I need some air."

I consider following her outside, but one look at Zoe tells me that I need to talk to her first. "What happened?"

"Isabel is just way, way too sensitive," Zoe says. Her face is pink along the brim of her nose and cheeks, which tells me more than her words. She is mad, and feeling guilty, and then mad at feeling guilty.

"It's all good," Shell says soothingly. "There are no accidents." Then a distinct look of un-zen-ness crosses her features. "Oh, crap. I'm losing it."

I pick up Shell's yoga mat and hand it to her. "We'll be okay in here," I say soothingly. "Maybe you need to meditate for a while?"

Shell looks at the mat as though I have offered her a, well, lifeboat of truth. "I just need fifteen or twenty minutes," she says, almost desperately.

"Knock yourself out," Zoe says.

"Thanks, you guys. I'll talk to you later, okay? We'll work it out. It's all ... " She shakes her head and leaves.

When the door is closed, Zoe mutters, "She is as flaky as a blueberry pie, isn't she?" She climbs her ladder awkwardly and plunks herself down on her bed.

"Yup," I agree, climbing up the ladder behind her. I sit at the end of the bunk with my legs crossed. "Okay, spill."

Zoe shakes her shiny, long hair so that it becomes a curtain she can hide behind. It's an old trick. "Nothing, honestly."

"Come on," I urge. "Just start at the beginning."

Zoe leans forward and tucks her hair behind her

ears with her good hand. "I arrived at the Fine Arts building for my session and Isabel was still there with a couple of her kids. So I waited and tried to get set up. It was pasta sculpture today."

"Macaroni art?" I clarify.

"It was on the schedule, so I'm trying to make the best of it, right? But then I realize that not only is Isabel late, she hasn't even followed the lesson plan. She's got all the paint out, and so now, on top of not having the proper supplies out, she's made this huge mess with paint and brushes and paper and easels. It's a total disaster. She's got them painting stuff like 'truth' and 'freedom.' Then my kids start whining that they don't want to do stupid macaroni art and the whole thing just gets out of hand."

"So, what did you do?"

"Well, finally, I just go up to her and say, you know, that it's time to clean up."

"And she got upset with that?"

"No," Zoe says slowly.

"So, what did she —"

"I'm not finished," Zoe snaps. "As she's cleaning up — taking her time, I should add — I say that maybe she should pay attention to the lesson plan ..."

"Huh?" Zoe was championing a lesson plan?

Zoe shakes her hair free and the curtain falls back over half of her face. "And that if she paid more attention to the rules, Cabin Seven probably wouldn't be falling so far behind Cabin Nine."

"Oh." I can practically hear the ka-chunk of little pieces falling neatly into place.

"What's that supposed to mean?" Zoe demands.

"It means, oh," I say. But it actually means a few things. As little as I know Isabel, I know that the battle of the cabins would be the last thing that would inspire her to change her ways. But what really seems strange is to hear Zoe — Queen of the Rulebreakers — coming down on Isabel for doing something that she herself wouldn't have thought twice about doing if only she'd thought of it first.

"So, let me get this straight. You were upset because Isabel was doing painting instead of macaroni art?"

"Pasta sculpture," Zoe corrects. "And she said it was lame, right in front of all my kids! How am I supposed to teach it when she's got her kids doing portraits of freedom, or whatever, and they're all covered in paint and having a great time? I'm supposed to make noodles fun after that?"

There it is. The invisible thing, as Isabel might say. Isabel had a better idea and it pissed Zoe off. End of story.

Right this minute, I get what Shell was babbling about when I entered the cabin. You can either grab hold of that lifeboat of truth or you can do what I choose to do now — stay with the big ship of easiness because it's easy, familiar and possibly has a satellite dish.

So, instead of asking her if she is mad at Isabel for having a better idea, I deal with the visible thing.

"Do you want me to talk to Isabel?"

"It won't help," Zoe answers. "She has it in for me. I don't know why. Well, actually I do. She's a freak and she's jealous of us."

Zoe and I have often used the jealousy defense for things that we can't explain, but I don't think it fits now. "Maybe. But the thing you have to know about Isabel is that she's got this real problem with conforming."

"So much for team spirit," Zoe says.

"Yeah, I guess. It's just that with Isabel, anything that isn't, I don't know, true, on the up-and-up ... drives her crazy."

Zoe looks at me like I'm babbling incoherently, possibly because I'm babbling incoherently.

"You're not really saying anything, you realize that?" she says.

"I know, I know."

"So, what are you trying not to tell me?"

Sometimes Zoe really nails things.

"The other day, Isabel and I were talking and she told me that her mom left a few years ago." I tell Zoe the whole story: the yoga instructor, the plumber, the facts as I know them. Zoe listens intently. "And then there was this thing with some friends of hers, Kelly and Shelley or Melly, or something. Anyway, it got ugly. I think that Isabel has a huge issue with honesty."

"When was I dishonest?"

"You weren't, exactly." I can't bring myself to tell Zoe that Isabel is ridiculously accurate at figuring out when people aren't saying what they mean. "I'm not saying I understand Isabel completely." Even as these words leave my mouth, another stupid lifeboat of truth sails away.

And, anyway, how do I know what the truth is? I wasn't there. Truth is tricky, hard to pin down. Truth is like Jell-O.

"Well, I'm not the only one who's getting tired of her," Zoe says. "She doesn't go out of her way for anyone except herself. And if she keeps it up, she's going to ruin the summer for everyone."

The door swings open. Charmaine and Jennifer walk in. "You guys coming?"

"Huh?" I ask.

"Cabin meeting," Charmaine offers.

"We're meeting at the fort. We have to go over some administrative details," Jennifer says importantly.

This probably means we'll be adding up points to see if we're ahead of Cabin Nine.

"Aren't you coming?" Zoe asks, following the others.

"I'll catch up later."

As they leave the room, Zoe throws me a look that tells me she's as miserable as I am. For a second I'm tempted to follow, but something holds me back. I need to find Isabel.

As the door closes and I'm left alone, I realize that at this moment I am neither on the lifeboat or the ship. I'm somewhere in between, treading invisible water.

Chapter Fifteen
Conjoined Twins Disjoined

I walk over to the Fine Arts building to see if Isabel is there. She is. She's sitting in a corner in front of an easel. Light filters in through a broken wood shutter and illuminates the lower part of her face. Her eyes are in shadow.

I stretch my neck out toward her painting like a cautious turtle. "Can I look?"

She shrugs.

I take this as a yes.

"I just started," Isabel says.

There are a series of charcoal lines on the heavy cream paper, not very many lines, yet the outline of a lifeboat, and in the distance an ocean liner, is unmistakable. I'm surprised and impressed.

I offer my expert artistic evaluation. "Wow."

"I've barely started," she repeats, brow creased. She adds another line and a blur with a brush of her hand, and then there's water — and it's angry.

"Huh," I say, thinking how many words it would take to say what her picture is saying. "Is the little boat heading to or away from the ship?" I ask, bending closer. "Is there anyone on it? Who's steering? The wind?"

Isabel shakes her head. "I don't know yet."

"Really?"

"Why?"

"I don't know. Isn't it inside your head?"

"Hmm," she says. She returns to her drawing. "I don't believe in knowing exactly how things are going to turn out, that's all."

I am a turn-to-the-end-of-the-book-to-see-how-things-are-going-to-turn-out kind of person myself. "I hate not knowing."

"Yeah," she says, not looking up. "I kind of figured."

"There's a meeting," I say abruptly. Suddenly I'm tired of everybody thinking they know so much about me — Karim, Zoe and now Isabel. And I'm tired of figuring out what everybody else wants. I'm tired of figuring in general. These are the things I want: a suntan, laughter, snacks, a cute boyfriend who laughs at my jokes and doesn't give me a teddy bear on Valentine's Day, friends, happiness. That's about it.

What I don't want are people who say things that make me crazy for wanting to know what they mean. I don't want invisible things. "I'm going." I move to the doorway. "Are you coming?"

She doesn't respond, but when I'm outside again,

walking toward the trail that leads to the fort, I hear the door to the Fine Arts building close.

"I am trying, you know," she says.

I bite my lower lip to keep myself from saying anything. I try to remember what I want: suntan, laughter, snacks. It's my new mantra. Shell says that if you say a word or a sound over and over, it connects you to the universe. I like this idea. It is more appealing than having to figure out what Isabel or Zoe or Shell wants. I would like to think that is the universe's problem.

We head toward the path that leads to Teacup Mountain. The fort is about halfway up the trail.

Inside the forest, the air is cooler and the ground is spongy. There was a light rain last night and it stripped the dust off every leaf and flower, leaving the foliage brilliant in a thousand coats of green. Sunlight threads its way through the canopy of leaves like ribbons of gold. Even though we haven't been speaking, we become quieter and quieter with each step until it feels like we're part of the forest, like it's inside us. We travel lightly, careful not to crack any twigs or rustle any leaves unnecessarily. Being here suddenly feels like a gift. When I look behind, I see that Isabel is standing in the middle of the path with her face raised toward a wider stream of light. She's gone somewhere else.

I think everybody needs a place to go when things become too much, a place where the world is the way you want it to be and, if you had the choice, it's how you would have created it. I go to water because everything feels spread out there, dissolved into the molecules that stretch across two-thirds of the world's surface. I think that Isabel's place is the forest, with its sheltering branches above and blanket of moss below, a place where light finds its way cautiously. Maybe one day I'll ask her if I'm right, but not today. I'm done with questions today.

I wait. When she opens her eyes finally, she looks at me, embarrassed. I shake my head and her face relaxes.

We're about fifty feet from the fort when I notice a strange sight. Charmaine is up in a pine tree. This is surprising because she is mortally afraid of ticks and Lyme disease and heights, and also because she should be at the meeting and not sitting directly above it eating a chocolate bar. I wave, but she doesn't notice. Too busy balancing and munching, I guess.

I wait for Isabel as we approach the fort. She points up to Charmaine with an amused look on her face.

At that moment, Jennifer's voice rings out clearly. "Her own mother left her?"

I hear Zoe's voice. "In the middle of the night. With the yoga instructor ..." Her voice dips below our ability to decipher and then rises again. "... Anna told me that she had this problem with some of her friends, Shelley and Riley, I think she said."

I turn, hoping that Isabel hasn't heard any of this. But she's right behind me, and her face has turned skim milk bluish-white.

"Isabel," I say.

"Kelly and Melanie. You really should get your facts straight." She turns and walks back down the path.

I hear a crack, a rustle of leaves and a very faint "Oh, poop."

I look up to see Charmaine scrambling down the tree with at least half of her chocolate bar wedged between her teeth. It dawns on me that she is the lookout, especially when she gives me a wild-eyed "oh no, we've been caught" look.

We walk into the fort together. Charmaine whispers "Sorry" to Jennifer and then tacks on "... that I'm late."

This is too stupid to ignore. "You were late for a meeting because you had to climb a tree and eat a chocolate bar?" I ask.

"Yes," she says, as she turns the color of ripe raspberries.

Zoe is in the corner of the room, guilt plastered across her face. "You didn't say not to tell anyone."

"I thought it was obvious."

Jennifer steps forward. "Zoe was just explaining Isabel's situation. She thought it might help us to understand her better."

It's funny how a lie can seem so reasonable when you're the one making it up, but so completely insulting when you're the one it's being handed to.

"How could you do that?" I ask Zoe. "Why did you do that?"

"Honestly, Anna," Zoe says.

"'Honestly, Anna'? That's it?"

"Can we talk about this outside?" She pushes past me, and I follow her away from curious eyes.

"What is the big deal?" she asks, once we're far enough away. "Technically, you didn't say I shouldn't tell anyone."

"I can't believe you're giving me the technicality argument!"

"Well, I can't believe that my best friend would embarrass me in front of a bunch of *extras*."

The term makes me cringe. We've always used it to describe, well, anyone other than us, basically. Now it just sounds cruel.

"I have to go."

"Anna. You have to stay and talk to me," she pleads. "I'm sorry. If you want me to be sorry, I'm sorry."

I hear this from a distance. The space is closing around me, and I know now why so many stories have enchanted forests. They force you to stay and wander in circles. Only the pure of heart ever make their way out of an enchanted forest. This makes sense to me. I begin to run.

By the time I reach the edge of the woods, my heart

is beating wildly, thumping in my ears. My palms are sweating and my breath is desperate. Once I'm outside the gates of the forest, I find a patch of sunshine. I stand still and inhale deeply. My breath comes raggedly at first, but eventually the world stops spinning.

I feel stupid. I haven't run away from bogeymen since I was ten years old, convinced that our freezer room in the basement was haunted.

I know what I need now: the sea. I head toward a secluded part of the beach so that I won't find anyone, and no one will find me.

But, as I'm rounding a corner to a quiet cove, I spot Shell. She's sitting in the Lotus position, facing the waves. Her wild hair is flying around her head like a cirrus cloud, and as she puts a hand up to hold it off her face, I see a cigarette in her hand.

Now, personally, I couldn't care less if Shell smoked. But it does seem odd that someone who peels tomatoes because of pesticides would willingly ingest over four hundred known carcinogens directly into her lungs. (I was paying attention to Constable Roberts last fall when he came to talk about drugs and alcohol. Very cute constable.)

Anyway, it's none of my business. I back away, deciding that a smoking Shell would probably be a very untranquil Shell. As I leave, I realize that I know next to nothing about her. And really, I know next to nothing about the rest of Cabin Seven, even the ones who have been coming here for years. They are, as Zoe said, the *extras*.

We never meant to be mean. We really didn't. It just meant that Zoe and I, together, were enough. We didn't need anyone else.

I remember now what Mom said before I came to camp, that maybe it was good for me to have some time apart from Zoe. How did she put it? "You've been acting like conjoined twins for years now."

Two people, but not completely. I wonder now if it's true.

"Just be yourself," she yelled as the ship left the dock. She said it like it would be enough.

Chapter Sixteen
CIT Scales Mount of Grunge

I find my own spot on the beach where I can listen to the rise and fall of waves against the sand. If I were wearing my bathing suit, I would dive into the water and everything else would be shut out. But I'm in sweatpants, so I decide to do the Shell thing and attempt some calming yoga.

I try to figure out the perfect pose. I'm not feeling peaceful enough for the Lotus position. I could do the Pose of the Child, but that would mean getting sand all over my forehead, so I decide on the Warrior pose. I stand against the rising wind. My legs stretched in a V, I raise my arms over my head. Slowly I turn and stretch my arms to the side. I bend until my right hand touches the sand. As I twist my neck upward so that I can see the fingers of my left hand, which are splayed against the pale blue sky, I see a face etched against the clouds. I scream and am suddenly the Shrieking Damsel as I crumple into the sand.

"Sorry," says Karim.

I sit cross-legged and try to think of a way to re-cover. "It's okay," I say.

"What were you doing exactly?"

I can't quite bring myself to say I was doing the Warrior pose.

"Nothing."

Karim sits down beside me in the sand and wraps his arms around his legs.

He looks at me sideways with one eye closed. "You look like you lost your best friend."

"That's because I lost my best friend."

He smiles because he thinks I'm joking, but then the smile disappears. "Isabel?"

"Zoe! How could you not know that Zoe is my best friend?"

"Sorry. I see you and Isabel together more often and you seem pretty comfortable with each other."

"You're right. I haven't been acting like Zoe's best friend. You're totally right."

"I didn't say that."

"But it's true."

"Listen, I don't know anything about you and Zoe, but I spent enough time with her last year at the pool to know that she has to be the best. People like that are pretty high maintenance."

"High maintenance?"

"Yeah. It's not a bad thing. It's not a good thing, either. It's just a ..."

"Thing?"

"Yeah, it's just a thing. High-maintenance people need constant attention. They're like foreign cars. Great to look at, but can you afford the parts?"

"My friend is not a car," I say. "Besides, the whole thing is my fault."

"Wow, you're pretty important."

"What's that supposed to mean?" I ask.

"It sounds like everybody's happiness depends on you."

"I didn't say that."

"You didn't have to."

"Do they teach this helpful stuff at counselor school?"

"No, they teach us to recognize pouting campers who want to sit around feeling sorry for themselves."

If there was any part of me that was still engaged in a crush, it disappears now. That sound? Crush flush.

"I'm not feeling sorry for myself. There's a difference between feeling sorry for yourself and genuine remorse."

"So, what have you done wrong?"

What had I done wrong? I told Zoe about Isabel's mom and her ex-friends. I hadn't paid enough attention to Zoe. I'd done everything wrong. But I'm not about to admit this to Karim, who apparently does nothing wrong.

"It really is none of your business." My voice sounds as empty as the crab shells scattered around me. "And it's kind of weird, don't you think, for you to be giving me advice on friendship? It's not like I ever see you hanging out with anyone."

The words flutter in the air between us.

"I thought I was hanging out with you." He gets up and walks away.

I know I should call him back. But what would I say? Sorry? That word has lost its meaning.

I move to the edge of the shore where the wind brings the smells of the outgoing tide. Kids are dotted along the widening strip, searching for sand dollars and crab shells and other sea treasures.

The first time I saw the ocean when the tide was out, I was disappointed. "It's just ground," I said to my mom. "Just muddy ground."

She told me to watch. Before long the flats were covered with herons, geese with their young, gulls of every size and color. "See! They're feasting," she said. "It was just hidden." We sat there for a really long time until I begged her to start my dinner. I had to ask at least three times before she heard me, before she came back from wherever she'd gone.

When my mom wasn't being completely normal, she was a little weird. She liked to paint. Not pictures — rooms. Grady and I would come home from school. She'd yell out "Pizza!" instead of her usual "How was your day?" and we knew she was painting again.

She'd crank up the music, Gipsy Kings usually. She had this pair of jeans and an old linen shirt that used to be white. They were covered with splotches of color: charcoal, yellow, blue, streaks of orange and red. I think she painted when she was sad; she didn't like being sad. (She said it made her sad.) Sometimes she chose some pretty stupid combinations — we've never let her forget her periwinkle and gold phase. Afterward, we'd sit in the painted room and eat pizza. One time, she said to me, "Are you ever surprised that you're here?"

I had no clue what she was talking about, but she didn't give up. "Doesn't it seem weird that we're even here?"

I think I said, "Where else would we be?" She liked the answer. She scooched over on her bum and gave me a big hug. A paint can tipped over — there wasn't much left, only a few drops. I was going to get a cloth, but she stopped me. "It's just in the corner. Let's leave it." Which was weird because she was normally a neat freak. "It's just a little bit messy. It's perfect." So we sat there in that empty room and we watched the paint dry in tiny speckles of spilled color.

Mr. Hong says that the people I write about aren't messy enough. He says people are never, ever that crisp or neat. He says I clean them up so much that they don't seem real.

Later, I head over to the swimming pool. I'm almost at the change-room door when I seriously ask myself if I am intending to go inside.

"Yes," I say out loud. I don't know what I'm going to say to Karim, but I feel bad about what happened at the beach.

I walk straight through the door and to the pool area. He's in the pool, swimming lengths.

I sit in the bleachers and watch him. The sun is low, almost set. A heavy moistness is in the air; you can practically taste the salt. Karim's arms and legs move rhythmically through the water, barely causing a ripple.

I see that he's slower than he was. Or maybe I feel it. His form seems unchanged by the injury, but, while the form is the same, the cost has been his speed. His body won't let him do what he once could.

It makes me sad to know this. I wish I didn't. I want to tell myself that it isn't true, that he isn't injured, that he's just taking it easy, warming up. Any minute now he'll burst forward and be the swimmer I remembered.

It seems unbearable that he won't be able to live up to the promise. He almost made the Olympic team when he was only fifteen.

With every lap he slows a little more, and then I see his form begin to disintegrate, and he stops. He stands up about five meters from the end of the pool. His left hand reaches out to massage his shoulder. The movement is rough and impatient. He looks angry.

Then he turns and sees me, and he changes. The anger is replaced by something else. It's not the I-mean-business Karim, or the untouchable Karim that I see when he's with the other counselors. The look I see now is completely naked, like the paper Isabel was sketching on, and the lines are equally obvious and stark. Violent in a way — bold dashes of truth.

I disappear into the change room.

The next morning, Shell leads the yoga class. She shows us a new pose, Half Lord of the Fishes pose. No one even giggles. Mostly we just follow along. When she delivers the usual "It's all good," it sounds kind of unconvinced. She asks what's wrong, but nobody volunteers anything.

Isabel does the poses quietly in the corner of the activity room we've booked for our daily classes. At first, there were a few spectators throwing out rude comments, but as we have become a regular morning fixture, they've lost interest.

Zoe and I didn't talk at all last night at dinner, and Isabel didn't even show up, which caused Jennifer to comment, but not as heartily as she would have in the past. Maybe she was experiencing a slight pang of guilt, although I wouldn't put money on it. Mostly we just sat and ate our chili. When Charmaine announced that she'd picked up a tick, we were relieved to have something to talk about. We decided it was a mole and that she'd probably had it for years.

"See, it's not even moving," Jennifer decided, after poking it with a fork.

Charmaine said "ouch," but seemed happy about the diagnosis.

No one said anything about what happened at the fort. It was like it never happened. I wondered if maybe the whole thing would just go away, like the effects of a bad dream. Sometimes you just needed a few more sleeps between you and the nightmare.

As Shell shows us the Tree pose, Zoe stands in front of me, trying to "be the tree," but it's a broken-limbed impression, pretty wobbly. Instead of focusing on a fixed spot, as Shell has instructed, I watch Zoe. But obviously there is a reason for not fixing your focal point on a moving target because when Zoe loses her balance, so do I.

But I don't have a cast to deal with. "Are you okay?" I ask.

"I'm fine." She wrinkles her nose from beside me on the floor. "Are we okay?"

I feel a huge whoosh of relief. I nod because I want us to be. It's like seventh grade, the first time I saw the Top Five Girls You Hate list. The list was un-signed, but we all knew a girl named Carrie was responsible. She had been the undisputed alpha female since kindergarten. I always thought it was because she had to repeat kindergarten and therefore had the heads-up on how life worked.

The list had an awesome power. The five unlucky girls on the list (Cindy S, Cindy D, Margaret, Tiffany and Mandeep) never really recovered. No one dared to be their friend. And here's the weird part (weirder, I should say): they didn't even want to be friends with each other. It was as though they believed what the list said even though they were on it. Carrie's word became the truth, and it made them doubt themselves. Or maybe the list confirmed what they had always suspected — if people really knew me, they wouldn't like me. Thankfully Zoe and I went to a different school the next year, but we heard that the old regime continued. We vowed that what happened to those girls would never happen to us. We'd always stick together.

Zoe smiles at me now from the floor. "Crazy glue," she says.

"Right. Crazy glue." But I can't get the power of the list out of my head. I know it was a lie, but that doesn't matter. That's how powerful lies were. Are. Not one bit less powerful than the truth, and maybe more.

I stretch my arm along the side of the wall and press my face against the wood paneling. I know that even though I didn't tell a lie about Isabel, somehow, still, the truth has been twisted so that it no longer holds its original shape.

I hear Shell's reminder to "breathe in, breathe out." Everything will blow over, I lie to myself. I just need to breathe.

Isabel and I end up on dish crew that night after supper — the most dreaded duty after cleaning the boys' bathroom. It involves a large spatula, an even larger tin can and leftovers that resemble toxic waste. Gross at the best of times, in stony silence scraping plates is intolerable. Finally I can't stand it, neither the slimy ooze nor the silence.

"I only told Zoe about your mom and your friends because I was trying to explain —" I stop because Isabel is giving me one of her X-ray vision looks. I peer deep into the wretched contents of the tin can, which is preferable. "I just wanted her to know why you act, you know … why you say the things you say sometimes."

"How do I act?" she asks coolly.

"You know … like, all …"

"All what?"

I get a little aggressive with my scraping, and suddenly the spatula is almost submerged in the primordial goo. "Oh, gross," I moan.

Isabel watches me fish the spatula out with my thumb and forefinger. I run it under the sink.

"Don't try to explain me, Anna. And don't try to explain yourself. People just do … what they do." She sounds tired. "Besides, I didn't come here to make friends."

We scrape for a while longer and the mountains of dishes are whittled down to rolling hills.

"Then why did you come?"

"Yeah, I'm gonna tell you. Cuz you're so trustworthy."

And then from nowhere, as usual, Marcus appears. Of course he doesn't walk up to us like a normal upright human being; he kind of serpentines across the room, looking over his shoulder like he's being followed. With one quick move, he hoists himself up onto the counter, takes a second to balance and swings himself over, almost spilling the gunk.

"Sorry about that," he says with a grin. "I need to work on my dismount."

"Hey, Marcus," Isabel says.

"Hey there, Girl of Many Colors. Hi, Anna."

"Marcus, we were in the middle of a conversation. Do you mind?"

"Oh, sure. I just wanted to see if you needed some help."

I consider taking him up on his offer. Isabel and I could go outside and talk privately. "Well —"

"Actually, we're almost done, Stuntman." Isabel gives him a rare and open smile. "I was wondering if you could show me that falling-out-of-the-tree routine."

"Oh, sure." He doesn't even try to hide his pleasure.

"That impact-preparedness move you were talking about might come in handy." She looks right at me. "You don't mind finishing up, do you, Anna?"

I force a smile. "Not at all. You two kids just run along."

Marcus practically skips out of the room behind Isabel. I am left with a Mount Grossmore of yet-to-be-scraped plates. Obviously Isabel is not a big believer in letting things blow over.

Chapter Seventeen
Visiting Day Arrives — Plot Thickens

The campers run around like maniacs the next day as they wait for parents to arrive. As each car pulls up, the din increases until the entire campground is a deafening maelstrom of noise. Big Jack greets everyone with equal enthusiasm and Old Betty stands beside him, trying out a smile for the parents.

My parents and Grady will be on the second ferry because of a baseball game, so I wander around watching the reunions.

Isabel is sitting with a man I assume is her father. He doesn't look anything like her, but then, unless his hair was ten different colors instead of thinning, he couldn't. Maybe the nose. Or the eyes? There might be a similarity there. I wonder if his eyes looked right through a person the way Isabel's do. My inspection of the eyes finally clues me in to the fact that they're both staring at me.

I decide to take a chance. "Hi, Isabel. Is this your dad?"

Isabel gives me a who-else-would-it-be look that I ignore.

Her dad jumps up, grabs my hand firmly and shakes it. "You must be Anna. Isabel wrote all sorts of nice things about you. I'm Davie. It's so nice to meet you."

I have to admit that I'm a little surprised to hear this. "It's nice to meet you, too."

"That was during the first week," Isabel explains.

"I had a particularly friendly first week," I explain to Mr. … er … Davie. (That's not really a Dad name, is it?) He just looks bemused.

"Why don't I get you girls something to drink," he says. "I'll be right back." He walks off in search of beverages.

I sit beside her. "I spent a whole hour finishing off the dishes last night, you know."

"A whole hour of dishes! I guess that makes everything all right."

"I guess you don't believe in second chances."

"I believe in catching onto things the first time, not waiting around for somebody to do the exact same thing to you again."

"I won't do the same thing."

She looks unconvinced.

"I'll … I'll do something completely different." A joke is risky at this point, I know. But Mr. Hong says that's pretty much what humor is for, to get you out of a jam. And it works now — Isabel's lips curl up in a smile.

"That's reassuring." She shakes her crazy hair at me.

"I am sorry."

"Yeah, yeah."

"So we're okay?"

She nods and says, "*We're* okay." Clearly this feeling doesn't extend to the others.

"What's that?" I say, pointing to an e-mail in her hand.

She folds it in half. "It's nothing."

"It's from your boyfriend, isn't it?" I exclaim.

"My boyfriend?"

"Yeah, your Swedish/Alsatian/Bosnian boyfriend who may or may not have royal blood flowing through his veins."

Isabel laughs, and I think it's the first time I've seen her teeth — in a happy way, that is. I feel hugely proud for this non-aggressive baring of teeth. "What are you talking about?"

"On the ferry, the first day? I saw you pulling that daisy apart, saying 'hates me, hates me not.' You know …" Isabel nods. "I assumed you had a fight with your boyfriend. But now you've made up, right? And he misses you desperately?"

"You really are a happily-ever-after gal."

"So?" I ask, pointing to the paper that she's folding into tiny squares.

She hesitates.

"I won't tell anyone."

"Not even Zoe?"

Now I hesitate. Anyone, in my mind, usually excludes Zoe. "Not even Zoe."

Isabel looks down at the paper and turns it over in her hands a few times. Then she unfolds it and thrusts it into my lap.

There are a lot of words, but basically the message is short. Isabel's mom is staying on Mayne Island, which is close by, and had been planning to come to Visitor's Day, but due to complications involving a Sven (plumber? yoga instructor?), she would not be coming.

"I'm sorry."

Isabel shrugs and takes the paper back. She gives me a look that is as naked as the one I'd seen on Karim's face the other day.

She tucks the folded paper deep into her pocket. "Hates me," she says quietly.

She looks lost, but only for a second. Then something crosses her face; it's not cold, exactly, just kind of not there. Neutral, I guess.

"I'm gonna go find my dad. Knowing his sense of direction, he's wandering on a cliff somewhere with two cans of pop, calling my name. You want to come?"

I'm about to say I should stay and wait for my parents, when I hear my name screeched out (slight exaggeration but only slight) and carried on the ocean breeze.

"That would be my mother," I say, wincing slightly.

Isabel smiles and leaves before I can tell her to wait.

It turns out it wasn't my mother bellowing, it was Grady. He races over, excited and yelling, but when he arrives he doesn't know what to do.

"Hi," he says, suddenly shy, flopping a hand up beside him that seems to have lost all cartilage function.

I give him a big hug. He warms up immediately and starts telling me all about the ferry and the awesome cheeseburger platter that he consumed.

Mom and Dad aren't far behind. Between them, I'm bombarded with news and feelings of home.

Grady's best friend's brother left for college. "His roommate has a snake tattoo," Grady says.

Grandma sent a care package. "She also has a snake tattoo," says Dad.

They say they met Shell already. "She has loads of freckles," says Grady.

"She seems very nice," says Mom.

"A little hippy-dippy," says Dad.

At the "hippy-dippy" comment, Mom gives Dad a hip check and I wonder if some of the planets have misaligned, causing a strange shift in my old solar system. They're on one planet. I'm on another.

"She is not hippy-dippy. I found her very interesting. She says she's teaching you yoga," Mom says.

"Mom's taking yoga, too," Grady shouts suddenly.

"What?" I ask. I draw them over to a picnic table and sit them down. "You're taking what?"

Now that I look closely, Mom does look a little … relaxed. And she's smiling in a benign sort of way. "Twice a week — and jogging. And I'm taking spirulina and wheat grass," she says proudly.

"Wow," I say. "My being away from home seems to agree with you."

Immediately she looks contrite. She reaches for another hug. "How can you say that? I've missed you terribly."

I harrumph at this, but I accept the hug and let myself enjoy the familiar smell of her perfume. Then I notice something.

"You got another hole in your ear?" I say, quite discreetly considering my surprise. When I wanted to get a second hole pierced two years ago, it was a major Hollywood production complete with tears (me) and yelling (also me).

My father, who doesn't know the meaning of the word discreet, says quite loudly, "And a navel ring."

My jaw drops. Honestly. Right down onto the sand — little sand crabs file in while I process this information. It's as though I'm at the scene of a grisly crime and can't keep from looking. To my immense, almost holy, relief her T-shirt is covering her stomach, but barely; it's teetering precariously on the rim of her shorts. If there were a sudden reaching emergency, all would be revealed.

"What do you think of this?" I go straight to my father.

"I think with all the navel-gazing she does, she might as well have something to look at." He shrugs. I should have known I wouldn't get a straight answer from him.

"Do you want to see it?" Mom asks.

"Good heavens, no." I actually say this.

My mom and I stare at each other. We've changed places. She's the giddy teenager and I'm suddenly the responsible, forty-something mother. We laugh, but a little uncertainly.

"Oh, sweetie," she says. She pushes me an arm's length away and begins the inspection. As she tells me that I've grown and need to be more careful with sunscreen, etc., I notice over her shoulder that Isabel is watching us. But when Isabel sees me, she looks away. She misses my wave for her to come over.

"Who was that?" Mom asks, twisting, not missing a thing.

"Isabel. I want you to meet her."

Mom turns thoughtful, but says nothing. Grady pleads with Dad to take him to the skateboard park. They take off.

"Show me your cabin," Mom says. She drills me with questions the whole way. "How is Zoe doing?" "How is your swimming coming along?" "Who are your cabinmates?" "Who is this Isabel?"

"Why do you say 'this Isabel' as if there was another one somewhere?"

"In your letters, especially the first week, you seemed intrigued by her. You haven't written much since Zoe joined you, so I was just curious."

"I'll write more," I say, even though this isn't what she wants. But I can't start with Isabel and Zoe. It's too complicated.

"How is Zoe doing?"

"She's fine."

She opens her mouth and then closes it again, and for a minute we walk in silence.

I grow suspicious. "Are you deep breathing?"

"Is there something wrong with that?"

"I guess not. You just seem kind of different."

She smiles. "When you come home, we'll go to a yoga class together, okay?"

I have a sudden flash of my mother giving me advice on how to do the very best possible Downward-facing dog and it's not a happy thought, but I stay quiet instead of saying "Fat chance," which I think is downright generous of me. "Here we are," I say, as we arrive at the cabin.

Thankfully there are loads of other people: Gin and her parents, Mags and hers, Jennifer's mom (her dad had to work, as he is a VERY IMPORTANT PERSON). The noise and tumult is good. It deflects my mom's questions, and I don't have to talk about Isabel or Zoe.

When it's time for everyone to leave to catch the last ferry, I look around again for Isabel. She and her dad missed the bonfire wiener roast, and they haven't been at any of the regular places.

"Maybe he had to take an earlier ferry?" Dad suggests.

"That's what happened," Mom decides.

They're probably right, but I feel like there might be more to it. I can't get Isabel's message out of my mind. If she thought her mom was going to be on Mayne Island, that was probably why she chose to come to this camp. Suddenly a few more things are making sense. The story is falling into place.

"I guess," I say.

Mom hugs me. "Have fun, okay?"

"Okay."

Then she whispers the same thing I've heard all my life. "Just be yourself."

I think about telling her to find a new cliché, one that's actually helpful. "Why do you always tell me that?" I say instead.

She looks surprised. She pushes my hair behind my ears even though, as soon as she takes her hands away, the wind blows it forward again. "Because," she says, "it's so easy to forget who you are, and because you are enough … and this being yourself business takes longer than I thought, and …"

"Mom, big breath. Right from the belly."

"It's just so … important …"

I stand up straight and lift one foot off the ground. "Okay. Tree pose." I wrap my arms, my limbs, around the trunk of me. "Big, strong, quiet Tree pose."

"You know, you're going to have a daughter one day." It sounds like a threat.

"Shhh," I say, eyes closed. "We are in the forest. We are the forest; we are the peaceful, unstressed, un-belly-button-pierced woodland. Bunnies frolic at our feet. Chipmunks scamper around our very roots …" I peek open one eye. She's so un-tree it's not even funny. But she is smiling.

"I like you," she says.

"And?" I let the pose go.

"That's it," she says mysteriously, or what she thinks will pass for mysterious. Then she tucks my bra strap into my tank top because she thinks it looks better that way. Neater. She gets a little glint in her eye. "You sure you don't want to see it?" She pulls her T-shirt up a fraction. I wince.

"I have never been more sure of anything in my entire life." Then I give her a hug. "It's not very appropriate, you know."

She smiles, lifts her shirt slightly and, before I can look away, my eyeballs are burned for life. She laughs out loud. "I'm rethinking appropriate."

"Watch out for infections," I call out as she joins Dad and Grady, still laughing.

I feel a twinge of loneliness at their leaving. I wonder how long it would take for me to be forgotten, for my place to be filled in — like a liver. You can take a whole chunk of the liver away and eventually it will regenerate itself. You'll never even notice that the old part is gone. Seriously.

Zoe joins me beside the gate. She sighs a huge sigh of relief as we wave good-bye. "My mother is nuts," she complains, pretending she has an eyelash in her eye and that's why she has to rub it.

"Mine, too."

We wave until the last van has disappeared down the long driveway.

Chapter Eighteen

Swimmer Stretches — As Far As She Can

It turns out that Zoe's cast is a bit of a guy magnet. Rock-climbing guy (Jake) and Skater-dude (Owen) have signed it with lavish understatement: "Hey, Zoe, Owen" and "Yo, Jake." Zoe is thrilled.

She shows me the signatures at the wharf after my swimming practice. She and I have been slipping a bit in our training sessions. Or, I should say, she's been slipping. I go out to the ocean every day, but mostly because it feels good and gets me away from the tension of the cabin, which is growing worse. Shell has run out of hopeful adages to guide us. Isabel and the other girls barely speak to each other, and I'm in the middle, which I hate — or in the water.

"What's happened to my keener coach?" I ask, taking my towel from her outstretched hand.

"Phht," she says. "You don't need me. Besides, there are bigger things, my dear. Much bigger things." She gives it the old dramatic pause. I wait.

"Jake and Owen want us to go kayaking with them after dinner."

"Really? Do they even speak? I've only heard them grunt."

"They talk just fine. So?"

I hesitate.

"C'mon. Jake says he thinks you're cute."

In Zoe land, this is grounds for true love. "Did he say that?" I ask, not completely immune to a compliment.

"Well, not exactly. But the way he looks at you is like he's totally into you."

"Hmm," I say, growing suspicious. It was more likely that Owen was into Zoe and I was some sort of consolation prize for monosyllabic Jake. I shake my head. "I promised Karim that I'd help out at the pool tonight."

"But lessons are during the day."

"I know, but a couple of kids need some extra help or they won't be graduating from Bottom-feeders."

Zoe's eyes narrow. "Like Isabel?"

"No, Isabel's doing fine."

"I hear she spends a lot of time at the pool. You think she's got a thing for Karim?"

"I — I don't think so," I stammer.

"Well, if she did, it would be the first thing about her that I'd understand. He's hot. Hey, are you okay?" she asks. "You're turning all red and blotchy. Did you get burned?"

I shake my head.

"Hmm. Maybe you're the one who has a thing for Karim. That's why you're blowing me off!"

"I do not have a thing for Karim." I lie so quickly that it surprises me. Wait. Was I really sure that I liked Karim? Maybe I didn't. So maybe, subconsciously, I was telling Zoe the truth. Maybe I didn't have a thing for Karim after all. That would solve a few problems. The most obvious one being that he didn't like me.

"Yeah, well, he's way too old for you anyway," she says, as if the idea is a bit absurd, even for her. "So you're really not coming?"

"I told him I'd help." I rub my face to hide the growing redness.

"You're always at the pool," she says. "We never spend any time together lately."

"Well, if you came to my swimming practices, we'd be spending lots of time together."

A little tinge of pink appears on both cheeks. "You don't need me. You'll be fine," she says.

"Really? You think I have a shot at beating Arlene?"

"Well ... sure," she says.

"That was enthusiastic. What did you mean that I'd be fine then?"

"Well, even if you're second, we'll still do okay in the overall points thing."

"So you don't think I even have a shot?"

Zoe straightens her shoulders and looks right at me. "I've never even beaten Arlene. Not really."

When I arrive at the pool, Karim is already in the water with Beverley. She's arguing about how she thinks the butterfly stroke should be done. He explains that she won't be trying the butterfly stroke until she can submerge her head in the water for five seconds.

I hear a chuckle from the bleachers and see Isabel. "That Beverley is a pistol."

"A real firecracker."

"Your family looked nice."

"I wanted them to meet you, but you disappeared."

"My dad had to catch the early ferry," she shrugs. "But you had a good time?"

"Yeah, I guess. It was nice to see them, but ..."

"But what?"

"I don't know. They just seemed like ... sort of more bonded, I guess. Connected. My mom got a navel ring!" I blurt out. "Can you even believe that? It's too gross. And when I get back, she wants me to start yoga classes with her!"

Isabel just smiles.

And then I hear my words the way Isabel has heard them. And I see the tiniest teardrop teeter at the edge of her eye. I place my hand on hers. I'm surprised that she doesn't move away. "Although," I add, "having your mother run away with the yoga instructor is probably worse."

There are at least a couple seconds of uncertain quiet before I know how she'll hear this. "Plumber," she says. Then there's a tiny snicker, and a chuckle, and we're both laughing like lunatics, holding our sides as the laughter comes in wave after wave.

As we dry our eyes with our towels, Jennifer's voice booms out across the pool deck. "Hey, Anna. Are you coming to the fireside?"

"Uh, yeah. After I finish up here."

"Okay, see *you* later."

I look over to Isabel. I hope she didn't notice Jennifer's slight.

"Don't worry about it," she says.

So much for not noticing.

"That's just Jennifer. If you don't do things her way she just loses all ..." I grope for words. "She just loses it."

"It's okay. I don't care."

"Do you really not care or are you just saying that?"

"Anna. When do I ever say something I don't mean?"

"Well, that's true. Why don't you care, then?" What I really want to know is, *How do you not care?* But I stick to my original version.

"Because I've been through this before. And I hate phonies. I don't do the sad story thing, okay? And you don't have to take care of me or fix me or anything. Really. I'm fine."

"Hey, Lipgloss, can I get some help over here?" Karim calls out.

I step out of my sweatpants. "I wish he'd make up his mind about which horrible nickname to call me," I mutter. "Are you okay?"

"Anna, what did I just say?" She says the words clearly and precisely, mocking me.

"Yeah, yeah. You're fine. I heard you. Is fine enough?"

She has no answer for this. She does, however, cock one eyebrow in an effort to look ironic and, maybe, nonchalant. But she looks young, like a kid trying it out for the first time — completely vulnerable, so easy to hurt.

As soon as I slide into the pool, Beverley insists on my personal instruction. Karim relinquishes control with a "good luck" smile over her head.

I grab a paddleboard and we do a lap together so that I can get used to the cool water. "How's it going, Beverley?"

"Okay." Her eyebrows are knit together as she concentrates on her kicking.

"Straighten your legs a little more. It'll really help you with your speed. Plus, you won't splash so much."

"I like splashing," she responds, flailing with even more gusto.

"Well, splash on your own time. The idea is to move gracefully through the water like a dolphin, not flop around like a shark's supper."

She giggles at this and I remember that she's just a

little girl, not a science-fiction mutant adult in a kid's body.

"So, how's the Talent Show coming along?" I ask.

"Much better," I say about her slightly reduced flapping.

"Nobody wanted … everybody wanted … never mind."

"No *King Lear*?"

She gives me a disdainful look that suggests I should have known this, and then adds, "Duh," in case I really haven't clued in.

Fine.

"You're eight, right, Beverley?"

"I'll be nine in January. I'm the oldest in my class."

Of course you are. "So, who's your best friend?" I ask, as I try to straighten out those legs. "The thing about swimming, Bev, is that you have to stretch. Stretch as far as you can; grab as much water as you can. And kick."

"Beverley," she corrects through gritted teeth. Then she kicks a little harder. "I'm trying."

"Okay, okay. Relax. So, who did you say your best friend was?"

"I didn't," she says.

As she struggles against the stroke, determined to do things her way, refusing to stretch so her limbs will work for her instead of against her, she reminds me of someone: Cindy S from the Girls You Hate list.

Carrie really had it in for Cindy. It wasn't enough that she was one of the top five most hated. After that, she was singled out for specific attention. I don't even recall what Cindy's great sin was, except, like Beverley, she was pretty vocal about her opinions. And then, of course, there was Hodgie.

Cindy had moved from Saskatchewan, and when she first came to our school, she was handed the "popular for a day" position that came from being a stranger and therefore mysterious. She talked about owning a cow, Hodgie, and belonging to the 4-H club, which seemed very glamorous, to us. She had raised her own calf, and we all begged her to bring pictures of it to school the next day. When she did, we clamored around her, anxious to see this Hodgie, whom we already passionately loved. He had a soft red-brown coat and milk-chocolate eyes. And when she told us that she loved him so much that her parents agreed not to send him to the butcher ... well, she was our hero.

I remember standing a little on the outskirts of the throng that surrounded Cindy. I could see Carrie pressing up next to Cindy, gushing along with the rest of the girls. Then she invited Cindy over to her house that afternoon to see her cat, Missy. To be invited to Carrie's house after school was a really big deal, and I thought Cindy would know this. But Cindy answered, "I told my mom I'd come home after school. Maybe some other time." She wasn't rude or anything; she actually looked like she wanted to go. And then she turned away from Carrie because somebody was asking her something, and that was the beginning of the end for Cindy. By the following week, the list was out and Cindy was at the top. By then we'd all heard whispers about how great Cindy thought she was and that all she could do was brag about her precious Hodgie. I never heard Carrie say it, but everyone knew that's where it started.

The death knell came from a little joke during math. The windows were open; the smell of a nearby farm wafted in. Carrie took a delicate sniff, said, "Whew, smells like manure," and at the same time she looked at Cindy and raised her eyebrows as if she was the cause. Everybody laughed. Ms. Neterbaum asked what was so funny, but no one answered. She chastised Carrie for speaking out of turn, but you couldn't punish someone for a look. It was the perfect crime.

Carrie circulated a petition after that (although no one ever saw her with it). It read "Cindy stinks." Every time you walked past Cindy, you had to hold your nose. We all signed the petition; we all held our noses. You had to or else you'd become part of the Cindy stink.

Cindy eventually became one of Carrie's most faithful followers, but she never looked the way she had those first few days, not to me anyway. It was like part of her went somewhere else — maybe back to Saskatchewan.

"Am I doing it?" Beverley is breathless after working hard on her stroke.

I force myself back to the present. Beverley's legs are as crooked as ever. Muscles are as stubborn as anything else.

"You're doing great, Beverley. You're really making progress."

She climbs out of the pool and sinks down onto the deck with her towel wrapped around her. "You can call me Bev if you want," she says solemnly.

"Really?" I scoop myself out of the water and plunk down beside her. "Like, for real?" I shove her playfully with my shoulder.

"Yes," she says seriously. "But only when we're here and only when no one is listening."

"It's a deal." I jump up and pull Beverley to a standing position. As I walk with her to the change room, I put my arm around her shoulders. "Good work today, Bev," I say. "Really great progress. Divine, really." She smiles. "Maybe I should call you Heavenly Bev?"

Her face contorts with a look that is somewhere between horrified and disbelieving. "Or not," she says gravely.

I walk back to Isabel and Karim, smiling.

"You're looking pretty pleased with yourself," says Karim. He's leaning on one of the bleachers with his muscular arms stretched out behind him. It isn't an unbecoming position.

I clear my throat, which makes an attractive phlegmy sound. "I'm happy with Beverley. She's coming along well."

"So are you, Lipgloss. She really responds to you."

I zip my jacket up so forcefully that I nick my chin on the zipper. "Thanks, but do you think we could skip the nicknames when the kids aren't around? Besides, I'm not even wearing lip gloss." I purse my lips out in what I hope is a defiant manner, although later I will allow that there is no effective way to purse one's lips in a defiant manner.

"Nice lips."

I retract said lips immediately and blush.

Then Karim looks a little embarrassed, which is only a slight consolation.

"Okay, well, I'm in the mood for a marshmallow," Isabel says, coming to the rescue. She collects me by the arm as she walks by. "Are you coming?" she asks Karim.

"No. Thanks, though. See you guys tomorrow."

I raise my hand in a farewell, but I can't say anything. The crush is back.

Damn.

When we're almost at the fireside, I turn to Isabel. "Do I look …?" I stop, not knowing how to finish the sentence. I know I'm blushing like an idiot.

Isabel grins. "Different?"

"No," I say with a frown. "Do I look different?"

She laughs and shakes her head. "You look soaking wet." She adopts a stage whisper. "People will think you've been swimming."

"Funny."

She gives me a sly look. "He does, you know."

"No, he doesn't."

"I think he does."

"Has he said?"

"To me?"

"Well, you're always talking to him. Anyway, I don't care. Forget I asked. It doesn't matter. Honestly."

"You're such a convincing liar."

"Am not."

"Am not a *convincing* liar or am not a liar? Either way — you are, too. If lying was a primary color, you'd be purple right now."

"Purple isn't a primary color. Red and blue make purple."

"Yes, that's what we're talking about, the color wheel. Not about how Karim likes you."

I practically slap my hand over her mouth and drag her over to the Honesty Tree. People are looking at us.

"That was really quite uncomfortable," she says, once we're safely in the shadow of the tree.

"Sorry. But Isabel …"

"Anna."

"Isabel —"

"Anna," she interrupts, smirking.

"I'm trying to tell you something."

She rolls her eyes and moves toward the fire. "I'm not going to tell anyone. Who do you think I am?"

I'm relieved to hear this, and I realize that I trust her completely. It doesn't even seem possible because I've known her for such a short time, yet it's true. Another of Mr. Hong's sayings (I should give him Shell's phone number; if anyone would appreciate his near-endless supply of sayings, she would) is that a journalist enjoys a license to be educated in public. And I wonder if Isabel is educating me in some way. It's not a comfortable thought.

Chapter Nineteen
History Repeats Itself ... Again

Cabin Seven has secured a position around the camp-fire. Isabel has gone to get marshmallows. Zoe is on a log between Jennifer and Charmaine. As I join them, Jennifer leans over to Zoe and Charmaine and whispers something. A cold shiver creeps up my spine. Jennifer glances over at me while she is speaking — the cold travels through me and twists itself around my heart.

Zoe looks stricken. Charmaine giggles and passes on whatever she's been told to Benita and Mags. It's like Broken Telephone, the game we used to play when we were little.

It used to be funny, but I'm not laughing now.

But this is Zoe, I tell myself. We're above all this intrigue. Crazy glue. Inseparable, no matter what the Jennifers or Carries of the world threw our way.

I force my legs to move forward even though Charmaine is laughing quite hard now. Benita and

Mags are smirking as well. Gin leans forward to get in on it, and Mags whispers something to her.

"What's so funny?" I ask.

Jennifer smiles. "Nothing," she answers. We could be back in elementary school with Ms. Neterbaum asking the same question. It's the identical sweet-smiled response.

"I'm thirsty," Zoe says bluntly. "Are you thirsty, Anna?"

I've been drinking from a water bottle since I left the pool and the nearly empty evidence is still in my hand. "Parched," I say.

We pass Isabel as we leave the group. She's carrying two sticks and half a bag of marshmallows.

"We'll be right back," I say, but Zoe clutches my arm and whisks me forward.

We don't speak until the bonfire is a distant shimmer. The moon is almost full and lends enough light to make our way down to the beach. It's quiet except for the slurping of waves on the shore and the thrum of noise from the campfire. There's an occasional squawk of a lone gull.

"What are you doing?" Zoe blurts out.

I glance around as though I'm missing a very important clue hovering just above my left shoulder. "Standing here?"

"Jennifer saw you."

"Jennifer saw me? What do you mean?"

"Why are you giving her ammunition? Don't you

know that she hates Isabel? The very first day I got here, do you know what she told me?"

"What?"

"That your market value was slipping."

Market value. Yup. That sounds like our future CEO. "Because of Isabel?" I say, filling in the blanks.

"Because of Isabel."

I try skipping a rock, but it's engulfed immediately by a breaking wave. "I know Jennifer doesn't like Isabel —"

"Hates."

"Okay, hates. But I haven't done anything to make her mad at me." I hear a tremor in my voice.

Zoe says nothing, and this makes me nervous.

"Are you saying I shouldn't be Isabel's friend?" I ask.

Zoe looks at me with narrowed eyes. "I'm saying you shouldn't go around holding hands with her."

"Holding hands?" I almost laugh. "*That's* what Jennifer is saying?"

"She saw you, Anna. At the pool."

I rewind my mental video camera and there it is: an innocent gesture, a simple reaching out, now distorted like a Broken Telephone phrase. The new truth. "You've got to be kidding. Isabel was upset. I was just reassuring her."

Even in the dim light, I can see Zoe's relief.

"What, you were worried that I suddenly turned lesbian?"

"Of course not," Zoe says. "But you know how

Jennifer can twist things around. First you didn't want to go canoeing with the boys —"

"And then I'm holding hands with Isabel. Obviously we're lesbian lovers. What else could it be?" It's the Omnipotent Carrie thing. If Jennifer goes public with this rumor at school, I might as well change my name to Cindy.

"We better get back. She'll be mad at me if she thinks I told you."

"You want me to pretend that I don't know?"

"I didn't say that."

"Well, what are you saying?"

Zoe's eyes skip across my face, and she looks past me.

"She told me in confidence," she finally says.

"What?" I explode. "The other day it was the technicality argument and now you're giving me the confidentiality clause? Since when are you and Jennifer so tight?"

"Since my best friend ditched me for an *extra*." Her eyes have no trouble locking onto mine now.

"I didn't ditch you," I say. "I've been busy with the swimming stuff and —"

"Is-a-bel."

"I never said that you couldn't hang out with us."

"Hang out with you? Gee, thanks, Anna. That's so generous. The only reason I came to camp with a broken arm —" she waves it around like a flag — "is because I thought ... oh, never mind." She starts to walk up the hill.

I catch up and grab her good shoulder. "What? You thought what?"

She doesn't turn around. "That you needed me."

"Of course I need you. Duh."

"No, Anna. Not 'duh.' You were fine, just like you always are. You always know how to take care of yourself. You never need anyone. At the hospital you sounded like you needed me. I thought maybe this time was different. But it wasn't."

I'm speechless. And when she walks away, I don't stop her. Instead I wonder how I could not know she felt this way. How is it possible not to know your best friend?

All the times I've been sad feel like nothing compared to this. But it isn't just sadness. I feel ... let go.

Isabel finds me sitting on a log, listening to the pounding waves. I don't know how long I've been out here, only that I'm shivering.

"There you are," she says, sitting beside me. "Where'd you go?"

"Here."

Isabel chuckles. "Well, sure." The crashing waves fill in the silence. Then she says, "You want to be alone?"

"Actually ... no. What's going on back at the campfire? What are they saying?" I hear that my voice sounds urgent, desperate, pathetic, but the idea that everyone is discussing me is gnawing away at my gut.

"What's the matter, Anna?" Isabel moves closer and touches my hand. I jump up as though she is acid.

She's the outsider, not me. But if I get too close, no one will be able to tell the difference — there will be no difference. And I will disappear.

How did this happen to me? The question is so loud in my head that I can't hear what Isabel is saying. I know she's saying something, but the words are sucked into a black hole.

My face feels hot and wet. I'm crying, but I'm numb. I'm numb and shivering and terrified. "Just go away, okay, Isabel? Just stay away from me."

She looks like I've slapped her. "You were right, Anna. You said you wouldn't do the same thing again. This was completely original. God, I'm an idiot." She walks into the darkness, and then I really am alone.

Chapter Twenty
Studies Show: People Suck

Shell calls a meeting the next morning after our yoga class — a class bristling with tension. Zoe wouldn't look at me; I wouldn't look at Isabel. Jennifer and I looked at each other, but not officially, which I only know because every time I checked to make sure she wasn't looking, I caught a trail of recent eye movement.

What if our looks had collided? Which one would I have offered? The groveling, let-me-back-in? The proud, I-don't-need-you? The offended, how-could-you-do-this-to-me? There were too many choices, and I had no one to run them past. Zoe was completely ignoring me and this had never happened, at least not in public.

Shell claps her hands. "Okay, you guys, we need to talk."

Gradually the room grows quiet.

"We have some business to discuss. First, the Talent Show is coming up. What do you want to do?"

"Do we get points for that?" Jennifer asks.

I close my eyes so that I can roll them in private. When I open them again, Isabel is looking at me. She knows exactly what I'm thinking. I shift so that I'm facing Shell directly.

"No," she answers smoothly. "This is strictly for fun. Cabin spirit." She snorts at this.

I steal a look at Zoe, wondering if she's remembering the "sprit" from her letter, but she isn't looking at me.

"Okay, forget the Talent Show. There's something else I want to talk about." Shell looks around the room. Her wild hair is bound back in a ponytail. Today's T-shirt reads "Budweiser, baby." "The vibe in this place is really, really heavy. I could barely sleep last night. Anyone want to talk about it?"

I do. A voice shouts inside my head so shrilly that I almost jump. But I say nothing along with everyone else.

Shell sighs. "C'mon, you guys. The only way we're going to clear things up is to communicate, talk — express ourselves. Remember, 'Only connect!'" She holds her arms up high, then pulls them down quickly. "I didn't make that one up," she says. "E.M. Forster," she says quietly. "C'mon ... someone?"

"Well." Jennifer looks around the room. "I don't know what you're talking about." Her eyes are wide and unblinking. "We've only got a few days left and, with the competitions coming up, I'm sure we're all going to pull together."

Shell takes a breath. "Some things are more important than winning, Jennifer."

"But if our cabin is the best, doesn't that show cabin spirit?"

"I suppose," Shell says.

"Especially if everyone tries their hardest," Jennifer adds. "If you ask me, the bad vibe in this room isn't from not communicating; it's from not caring ... It's from atrophy."

I close my eyes again and bite my lip. She means apathy — not caring. I actually find myself uttering a prayer that Isabel will not correct her. If she makes things worse for herself, she makes them worse for me.

Isabel meets my gaze.

"Good word," she says, her tone free of sarcasm. "Atrophy. A decline."

Jennifer seems confused at this definition and with Isabel's apparent compliance. Isabel has picked up her book and is heading out the door, offering no explanation. But she doesn't need to. "A decline" is exactly what is happening.

Zoe is on her bunk beside mine, but she might as well be halfway across the world.

"Freak," Jennifer sneers, as soon as Isabel is out the door.

Shell doesn't say anything and, after picking up her yoga mat and rummaging through her drawers for something (I assume it's the cigarettes), she too is out the door with a weary "See you at lunch."

"Who's coming out to the archery course to practice?" Jennifer asks.

There is a chorus of "I wills," Zoe included, although she will be as helpful as an eel at a juggling contest.

"I should get some swimming practice in," I say, chancing a meaningful glance at Zoe. She can choose to come with me. It will be Jennifer-approved if she comes as my coach. But Zoe doesn't even look my way.

"How's it coming, anyway?" Jennifer asks, as if the night before never happened.

"Good. Fine," I say. You cold-hearted bitch, I think.

"Keep it up," she says.

"Okay, thanks," I say. Anna, you craven coward, I think.

I watch them take the path through the woods to the archery course. The sound of their voices hangs in the air long after I can't see them anymore. I try to hear Zoe. I'm relieved that I can't hear her distinctive laugh, and then I feel sick that I'm glad my best friend isn't laughing.

People are hard, I decide. Imaginary friends are easier.

Most kids have had imaginary friends at some point. Mine was Bea. I don't know what she looked like or sounded like. I guess you could say I felt her. We had tea parties and teddy bear picnics. She sat beside me at mealtimes and participated in all the regular imaginary friend activities. Sometimes she put up a fuss about not getting enough sugar for her tea or she'd want the last cookie (which I always took), but apart from that we got along really well. She was reliable and accepting and loyal, a stand-up kind of friend. But then I went to kindergarten. During our Friendship Circle, David Benchley tried to sit beside me. Without thinking, I told him that he couldn't sit there.

"You aren't allowed to save places," he said.

"I'm not saving a place."

"Then why can't I sit here?"

"Because Bea is already sitting there."

"I just told you, you're not allowed to save places."

"I'm not saving a place," I repeated. "Bea is already sitting there."

That's the way the conversation went until the teacher came over and asked what the problem was. I explained that my friend Bea was already sitting there. She just said, "Oh."

Absolute understanding permeated my brain with that "oh." Bea was not real. Bea did not exist. I was horrified. Then I was embarrassed.

Numbly, I said that David Benchley could sit there, which he did with an outstretched tongue, which got him banished from the Friendship Circle. The glee that I might have normally felt at seeing him punished was wiped out by the awareness that Bea was gone. And I had sent her away. I knew this even though I could never expect anyone to understand. I had sent my best friend away.

When I arrive at the water's edge, Arlene is swimming, tirelessly, it seems. She is half human, half dolphin.

She is streamlined. There are no wasted motions. Everything works together. I'm wondering what her weaknesses might be, when Shell sits down beside me.

"You're as good as her, you know."

I squint one eye against the bright sunlight. "Not nearly."

"How do you know?"

"Because she beats me every year?"

Shell shakes her curls. "No," she says abruptly. "That's not how you tell. This isn't about Arlene."

"It's a race," I explain. Maybe in Yoga land they don't have competition, but in the real world they do. "Only one person wins."

"Ha," Shell says, as if this is an appropriate response. "You want to go for a walk? I'm dying for a butt. I know I shouldn't smoke in front of the CITs. Bad influence. But I figure I couldn't suck any more at being a counselor then I already do, so what the hell, eh?" The wind dances a slow waltz with a curl in front of her left eye. She pulls the strand back. "Guess I shouldn't say that, either. Oh, well. Bad counselor."

"No, you're not," I say, but Shell is walking quickly and I don't know if she's heard.

The seashells crackle beneath our feet, and the smell of trapped seawater rises up. A few hours earlier, when the tide was in, all this would have been submerged, and now I'm crunching about on top of it. When you think about it, it's unnatural to live in the open air half the time and under water the other half.

As soon as we round the corner, Shell grabs her lighter and cigarette and, after a few unsuccessful tries, lights up. I watch as her eyes practically roll back in her head with pleasure. I have mixed feelings of awe and disgust.

"It's a horrible habit," she says unconvincingly.

"You're not a terrible counselor," I say, in case she didn't hear me before.

"I didn't say I was terrible. I said I was bad, and I am."

"No, you're not," I insist, not quite sure why.

Shell smiles. "Thanks, Anna. That's nice of you."

Either she doesn't really think it is a nice thing to say, or she doesn't think I mean it. I'm not sure which.

I pick up a round stone and rub it against my shirt. I stick it in my pocket.

"What are you thinking?" she asks.

"That people should come with headlines to let you know what's going to follow."

She laughs. "That would be nice." Then her smile fades. "You know what the worst thing is, Anna?"

"What?"

"Finding out that you're not original. One day you wake up and you realize you're just like everyone else — you don't know anything more than anyone else." She throws her cigarette down, grinds it against a rock with her foot and then bends and carefully gathers up the fragments. She sticks them in a Ziploc bag she must have brought for this very purpose.

"But you're not like everyone else," I say. "You are original."

"You don't have to say that, Anna. You don't have to make me feel better. I don't really mind feeling this way — it's actually a bit of a relief."

"What do you mean?"

"I was really excited about coming here this summer. I didn't love high school, to tell you the truth. It's pretty ruthless. I thought maybe, since I'd been through it, I could help — you know, offer up my great twenty years of experience. I thought I could just be real with you guys. But I forgot that when you're fifteen, man, you don't listen to anyone except the group. The group rules."

"But we — we've listened to you," I say feebly. "I really like your laughter saying. You know, 'Laughter is a shortcut to the soul.'"

Shell smiles. "It's not enough." Then she shakes her mane of hair. "I hated myself in high school. But not right away."

Okay, here comes a story. I should have my pen ready, at least in my mind. (Shut up, Mr. Hong!) But I don't want to hear her story. Too late — she's already talking.

There was a boy, she says. Maybe there's always a boy. His name was Nino. Foreign-exchange student, she thought, but not really. His family was from Toronto, but still, he moved to Shell's little town in northern British Columbia. He was exotic to her. He was cute and quick and funny, and he made her feel unusual. (Unusual. I feel myself being drawn in.) Just before Nino, Shell had a best friend named

Catharine. They were best friends since forever.

Catharine was also cute and quick, and she fell madly in love with Nino. He liked her, too. He liked her curly red hair and the way she walked in her running shoes and how she always looked a little bit lost. He didn't make Catharine feel unusual; he made her feel found.

A dilemma. (This is what I write on the notepad in my mind. What is more important: to feel unusual or to feel found? They both sounded equally critical to me.)

Shell says she convinced herself that she was the one who was meant for Nino. (Unusual beats found.) She was convinced that he needed her, too. So, she told lies to him. Lies about Catharine: her curly hair was a perm, the red was really mousy brown, she practiced that walk and she wasn't so much lost as found by a couple of previous boys. The lies were true, but that didn't matter. Nino lost interest and turned instead to Shell.

This isn't quite how Shell tells the story, but it's the way I hear it. And of course there's no happily ever after. He moved back to Toronto.

"I lost my best friend," she says. "Over a boy who moved away."

And the moral is? I want to ask. *What do you give up for what you think you need?* But it isn't my story; it's hers. "But you loved him?"

She snickers. "Hon, love had nothing to do with it. Sometimes people just suck."

Waves crash, gulls cry, crabs mutter whatever they mutter beneath the sand.

"Sorry, kid," she says. "I'm just having a bad day. Are you okay?"

"I'm fine."

"Are you sure?"

"Yeah, really."

"Right," she says, and I can see that she doesn't believe me. "Hey, look at it this way: camp's almost over. Pretty soon I'll just be a strange memory of some weird camp counselor you once had." She takes a few steps. "Crap, that was sort of a saying, wasn't it?" She shakes her head and jogs up the beach.

I go for a swim. I swim until I'm too tired to think. Zoe, Isabel, Shell, Arlene, Jennifer, Karim all meld into one amorphous blob of stuff that sucks. With every stroke and kick and pull, the blob disintegrates until there is nothing but the sound of my own breath, the blood pounding in my ears and the heartbeat of the ocean itself.

I realize something.

I am real here.

Chapter Twenty-One
... And Kick

Zoe is waiting for me outside the cafeteria when I arrive, dripping wet, for lunch.

She gives me a perfunctory up and down. "Aren't you going to get dressed?"

"I don't want to bring the wrath of Jennifer down on Cabin Seven for being late."

"She's not that bad."

I run a towel over my hair, which serves the dual purpose of making me less soaked and allowing me to emit a low growl.

Zoe pulls the towel up and peeks beneath. "Really, Anna. She has nothing against you. She likes you."

I yank the towel down around my neck and hold on to the two ends for ballast. "Why does what Jennifer think mean so much to you?"

Zoe's eyes fill with tears, and for a second I wonder if they are drama-class tears. But then she sniffs in a very unpoetic way, almost a snort, and looks embarrassed. "You don't have a clue what it's like for me here, do you?"

"I know you're sad that things are different."

"Oh, that's brilliant," she says, drying her tears with the sleeve of her shirt. "Sometimes you're so dense."

"Brilliant or dense? Make up your mind."

She waves her cast at me. "I can't *do* anything. I'm just an extra." She looks at me straight on.

It dawns on me then that Zoe is used to doing. For her, not being able to do anything was like plucking the tail feathers off an eagle. She was used to soaring.

I want to say something to make her feel better, but I get stuck trying to figure out what I really want to say, and I wonder if it's related to Isabel's "invisible thing" theory. Wouldn't it be weird if the real thing ended up being the invisible thing?

Maybe I just needed to rub my head a little harder with the towel.

Jennifer sticks her head out the cafeteria door. "Have you guys seen Isabel?"

"No," we say at the same time.

"Well, come in. Maybe they won't notice she's not here," Jennifer clucks like an old mother hen.

And, like two stupid baby chicks, we follow her inside.

I wake up the next morning with a feeling of immense relief. Today is the competition day, the last day of camp. Tomorrow we will be going home and, like

Shell said, this can become just a bad memory of a strange experience. Fine with me.

Last night I endured a painful bonfire evening of Amazing Jennifer stories. I smiled and nodded and laughed in all the right places along with everyone else. Isabel sat with Marcus and Karim at the opposite end of the fire. I tried to ignore the little Shell voice inside my head saying, "the group rules." When it came right down to it, there were far too many people giving me telekinetic advice these days, and I decided I needed to figure out a few things on my own. One of the things I'd already come up with was that life does not always turn out the way you planned. So what if this was supposed to be the best summer of my life. It was actually the worst summer of my life. Guess I got it wrong. So what? Time to move on.

There were two more weeks before school started. Zoe and I would make up, become strong again.

This was my plan.

I start the day with a swim, but nothing too strenuous. Steel gray clouds sit heavily on the horizon. Arlene is also there, and for a while we are in the water together. Very civil. It occurs to me then that there are going to be other competitors; a couple of girls from her cabin are also swimming. But we both know it's going to be the two of us. And that Arlene is going to win.

There is no swimming instruction today because everyone is decorating the camp for the afternoon competitions and tonight's Talent Show. Beverley is flying around looking very official in her capacity as decorating coordinator. She is, however, alone.

"Isn't anyone helping you?" I ask.

"They're supposed to." She shrugs.

"How's it looking for the Talent Show?"

"We're doing the Spit Skit." She pulls a face and then spies someone who is supposed to be helping her and she's off, struggling to hold on to an armful of supplies.

At the cabin, Charmaine is up a ladder decorating the outside of our cabin with fir boughs and wild flowers. Jennifer, Mags and Zoe are below giving instructions. (Did I mention that there are points for best-kept cabin?)

I go inside and get dressed. I notice that Isabel's bunk is neater than it has been. I wonder if she has decided to jump on board the *S.S. Competition* before it sets sail. This strikes me as unlikely since she's been almost completely silent for the last couple of days, but you never know. I go outside and join the worker bees. "Can I help?" I ask.

"Sure," Jennifer says, handing me an armload of branches and a string. "Make a wreath or something."

I have an urge to tell her that maybe she could stick the branches somewhere else, but Zoe catches the look on my face and says, "I'll help you."

This cheers me a little.

We fuss with the branches and soon we're laughing, mostly about how inept I am with a glue gun. It feels good. "Are we even supposed to have this thing?"

"I smuggled it out," she says, pointing to her sling.

"See, one of the benefits of a broken arm."

Zoe gives me a "very funny" grimace and things are starting to feel almost like normal, when Shell enters the cabin and comes out again almost immediately.

"Has anyone seen Isabel?" she asks.

There is a murmur of responses, mostly involving the word "no." "She was at breakfast," I say.

"That was three hours ago."

"Why do you want to find her?" Jennifer's voice sounds weird.

"The handyman thought he saw a camper leave the front gates with a backpack. He figured she was going hiking, but he said something about crazy hair and I had this feeling that it might be Isabel. Her stuff is gone. Did she say anything about leaving early?" Shell's tone has gone from curious to concerned to freaked out. "Jennifer?"

"Why are you looking at me? I hardly talk to her. The girl is unstable, Shell. You know that. How do I know where she went?"

While Jennifer is talking, I notice Zoe's face has gone blotchy.

"Have you checked the Fine Arts building?" I know that Isabel won't be there, but I need a diversion.

"Will you check?" Shell says gratefully.

"Sure. Zoe, come with me."

"I should stay here and finish up," she says, but changes her mind once she sees my glare.

We walk quickly toward the building. "What's up?" I ask, as soon as we're out of earshot of the others.

"Nothing."

"Zoe?"

She stops walking. "Honestly, I have no idea where she went."

"You know something, don't you?"

She looks like she wants to say something, but stops. She checks behind us like she's afraid we're being tailed.

"Does it have something to do with Jennifer?"

"I promised I wouldn't say anything."

"Zoe, you have to tell me," I say, calmly, like a paramedic talking somebody off a ledge.

"But Jennifer swore me to secrecy. You know what she's like, Anna."

Now is not the time to get into the long-tentacled reach of Jennifer, so I take a very deep breath. "If Isabel has left the campground without permission, it's not going to look good for anyone in our cabin. They'll probably dock us a thousand-million points. Maybe I can find her before anyone finds out."

Zoe looks down at her fingernails. "Nobody ever meant for her to leave."

"What happened?"

"Charmaine and Jennifer found this e-mail from Isabel's mom saying that she couldn't make it on Visiting Day." She lowers her voice. "It was just a joke."

"What was just a joke?"

"They had a friend at home send another e-mail to Isabel. I don't know exactly what it said."

"Just a joke," I repeat. "What did it say?"

Zoe hesitates.

I wait.

"That she wanted Isabel to come and visit her."

"Wow," I say. "Where's the punch line?"

"Anna, it wasn't my idea. I didn't even know anything about it until it was done."

"No wonder Isabel left."

"There isn't a regular ferry during the week. She's probably still on the island."

"Tell Shell that I went to look for her, okay?"

"Anna, the race is in, like, two hours. Everybody's counting on you."

"I'll be back in time."

"Don't be late."

"I'll be back," I shout over my shoulder. I go to the pool. If Isabel has said good-bye to anyone, it would be Karim. As I run, I can't help feeling the adventure of the moment and sort of, I don't know … heroic. I could be a hero.

He is at the pool, cleaning up the streamers from the day before when the younger campers had their races. He doesn't notice me come in the side entrance. It looks like he's favoring his shoulder as he pulls in the ropes and buoys.

"Hey," I call out. "Have you seen Isabel?"

"Not since last night. What's up?"

"She didn't even come by this morning?"

Karim stops what he's doing. "What's going on, Anna? Shell was just here and then flew off without telling me anything."

"Some girls pulled a stupid prank on Isabel, and I think she's left. All her stuff is gone and the handyman thinks that he saw her walking out the front gates with a backpack. Do you know when there's a ferry today?"

Karim glances at his watch. "They don't have a regular run on weekdays. I can probably still catch her."

"We."

Karim shakes his head. "Uh-uh. No way. Campers aren't allowed off camp property without permission. In fact, I should probably track down Big Jack and tell him about this ..." He hesitates. "I don't want to waste time." He walks to the garage and seems surprised to see me climb into the passenger seat of the truck. "Didn't you hear me?"

I look straight ahead. "Not really."

Karim sits there, not moving. "I can't leave with you, Anna."

"And you can't go without me. Sheesh. Big dilemma."

We sit there for a few seconds longer. Finally he exhales loudly and turns the key. The engine starts with a chug then a roar, belching smoke out the exhaust pipe. In minutes we're outside the camp gates.

We travel on gravel until we reach the curvy road that takes us to the main highway. Dark clouds are gathering just above the trees; the wind is picking up.

"Why do you think she left?" Karim says.

"Because of a stupid prank. Why do you think she left?"

He gives me a sideways look, and then he watches the road again, but it's enough.

"You think she left because of me."

He shrugs. "What do you think?"

"Listen, I was really nice to Isabel. When nobody else was being nice to her, I was. Zoe is my best friend. Was I supposed to turn my back on her? This wasn't exactly an easy summer for her either, you know."

"The problem wasn't that you weren't nice enough to Isabel. She didn't need you to be nice. She needed a friend."

So he knew about the day on the beach, how I told her to stay away. Isabel must have said something. "It's not that simple," I say quietly. "Zoe is my best friend."

"Who wants to keep you second best."

"No, she doesn't," I say adamantly. "You don't know what you're talking about."

Karim slows the car to take a curve. The wind is increasing and I can feel it push against the truck as we head toward the terminal. The ocean comes into view and it's eerily pale, mossy green. As the waves crest, you can see the translucence of the water just before it's tossed against the shore.

"I do know that you could swim circles around her if you let yourself. When you and Zoe did laps last year, you actually looked around to check if you were ahead of her. You paced yourself to swim slower."

I shake my head. "That's not true."

"And even this year, even though she's not swimming, you're still holding yourself back."

"This isn't about Zoe, okay? We were talking about Isabel."

The clouds open up. Big, heavy drops plunk down on the windshield, drenching the dusty glass. Karim turns on the wipers and suddenly everything smears together. A hundred shades of gray surround us: the sea, the sky, the highway. Tall cedars sway above us, decapitated by the mist.

"Isabel could have made an effort with everyone else, too, you know. It cuts both ways," I continue.

"Why do you think she was trying to swim?"

"It is a water camp, Karim."

"So what? She was totally terrified of the water, Anna. When's the last time you were totally terrified of anything?"

"That's a stupid question."

"Funny how it's a stupid question when you don't have an answer, which you normally do, by the way."

"It's a stupid question because it just is."

"Try answering it anyway, just for fun."

"People are supposed to avoid scary situations. That's why fear was invented, so that people would say, 'Guess I better head in the opposite direction and save my butt.' And you know what? Lots of saber-toothed tigers and woolly mammoths were avoided that way. Big, huge, helpful fact. Fear is a warning sign. STAY AWAY."

"Thanks for the anthropology lesson. When was the last time you faced something you were totally terrified of?"

"When did you?"

Karim pulls the car into the passing lane to overtake a farm vehicle. I wonder if I've stumped the unstumpable Karim. But when the steady drum of rain is the only sound in the car, I'm kind of sorry. It's left me with too much thinking space, and my thoughts keep flipping back to Karim's comment. *What she needed was a friend.* This doesn't have anything to do with being terrified. At least I don't think it does.

I've always thought of myself as a pretty good friend: loyal, supportive, true-blue. But I wonder if, objectively speaking, this is so. *The unvarnished, unbiased truth. Just the facts, ma'am.* (Thank you, Mr. Hong — obviously returned from his Hawaiian vacation.)

I consider the evidence.

Exhibit A: I ignored Zoe's needs at camp.

Exhibit B: I ditched Isabel as soon as it got tough.

Exhibit C: I chose to obey Omnipotent Carrie and was mean to Cindy S.

Exhibit D: I turned my back on Bea, my invisible friend.

In summary, not a great history of friendship, although I'm not sure that Exhibit D would hold up in a court of law. Still, it goes to motive. The conclusion is unavoidable. When it comes to friendship, I pretty much suck. *Sometimes people just suck.* Thank you so much, Shell.

"Coming here," Karim says abruptly.

"Excuse me?"

"Coming here this summer. That's the last time I did something that scared me."

"But you've been coming here for years."

"I learned to swim here when I was a kid. My first race was here."

"You won all the races." His name was on most of the trophies in Big Jack's office.

"Pretty much."

"What happened? With your shoulder, I mean."

"Nothing. And then … everything. It was over in a second. I was feeling a little sore, but nothing out of the ordinary. I had a big race that day. Really important. I did my stretches, thought I'd be okay, you know, swim through it." He smiles a smile that holds no joy. "Then it tore. It felt like the muscle just ripped itself away from the bone, and I knew it was over. I thought, This can't be happening. This is me; this is what I do. This is who I am. And then it was over."

"But injuries heal. Physio, surgery … It'll just take time, right?"

"The injury healed, but the speed is gone. One stupid second; that's all it took."

I don't know what to say. I'm fairly sure that I'm

on the brink of Isabel's invisible thing, but the problem with invisible things, obviously, is that you can't see them.

"I guess I thought something would change. You know ... magic." He laughs. "It was always magical here. But that's why I was scared — I guess I knew."

He passes another car and the spray sends a film of mud across the windshield. Karim turns the wipers on to full speed.

"The worst thing is disappointing everyone. My family — I have a big family — and my girlfriend. Everyone expected me to be something, to go somewhere. And suddenly I was nothing, going nowhere."

"Girlfriend?"

"Ex-girlfriend."

My heart does a little back flip at the addition of the "ex." (Ex marks the spot, Zoe would say.) And then I remember that my shaky-friendship trial is still in progress. "She dumped you because you hurt yourself?"

"Something like that." He shrugs. "So what's your scariest thing?"

"I don't know. I'm not avoiding the question, Karim. I don't do scary things."

And then the most silent silence of all descends.

At the terminal, Karim parks the truck. There is a ferry in the slip and I try to see, through sheets of rain, if anyone is standing on the deck. Even in this weather, Isabel's hair would be easy to spot. But as we run toward the ticket booth, the horn blows and the ferry pulls away. And that's it. We watch it maneuver out of the small harbour. There's no dramatic moment, no running up the gang plank (or whatever it is) and taking a bold leap across the ocean — a perfect arc — and landing at Isabel's feet. No reconciliation or redemption, just the rain falling on our faces as we watch the ship grow smaller and smaller.

Karim suggests a cup of hot chocolate across the street at the diner.

I didn't think it would turn out this way. I pictured Isabel sitting in the small, ugly waiting room. I would arrive just in time. We'd talk, straighten everything out. I'd tell her that those girls were wrong to send the e-mail. I'd stand up for her, and then we'd return, triumphant, heroic.

Suddenly there's a long, hard blast of a truck horn and the screech of brakes. A deer, maybe? A dog in the middle of the road? At the same moment, Karim grabs my arm and pulls me to the shoulder. The truck slows to a halt and pulls over.

The driver leans out his window yelling, "Are you okay?" That's when I realize that I am the one who was almost the dog in the middle of the road.

"I'm sorry," I stammer. "I'm okay."

"You be careful, young lady," he chastens me with the wag of a beefy finger. "You take care of her," he says to Karim.

"I'm trying, man," Karim says tiredly.

I wave good-bye to the man who was nice enough to not kill me and walk inside the diner. I know I should thank Karim. I know it, I know it. But I'm trying to think of a way to say it that will sound genuine because part of me thinks I would have seen the truck in time.

I open my mouth to say thank you, but what comes out is "I would've seen the truck."

Karim looks at me in disbelief. I look away, embarrassed. And that's when I notice a girl sitting in the corner booth. Only the top of her head is visible. But it's enough.

Chapter Twenty-Two
Girl Tells Invisible Story

She waves us over. She doesn't seem surprised that we're here. When we get to her booth, I can see why. She's had a nice view of my near death, a front-row seat, so to speak.

"Are you okay?" she asks.

I nod, embarrassed.

"Good save," she says to Karim, and then I really feel like snail scum for not thanking him.

"It wasn't really necessary," he says. "Apparently Anna had it under control."

"Okay, okay," I say. "Thank you, Karim. Thank you for saving my life."

"That's nice," he says. "I'm going to go over to that pinball machine. Come get me when you're ready to go. And don't be long. We have to be back in an hour for the races."

Isabel watches him go. "I see things are going well with you two."

"Don't even," I say. "So, what's with the backpack? And you ... here."

"You want something? Hot chocolate?"

"Yeah, sure."

Isabel waves to the waitress like she's an old regular. "Hi, Sheilah, could you bring us one more hot chocolate?"

"Sure thing, hon."

Isabel smiles. "I love this place. Everybody calls you 'hon.'"

"Isabel," I try again. "What's going on?"

She points down to the newspaper in front of her. "There's a story in here about this mother duck. It's kind of interesting. This guy was walking in the park and a duck waddles up to him —"

"Is this a joke?" I ask. "Does the duck walk into a bar?"

She wrinkles her nose, which is a no, I guess. "The duck sidles up to him and grabs his pant leg, pulling on him. He shakes it away, thinks the duck is a little goofy, I guess, and keeps walking, but it follows him and does the same thing again."

"Maybe it was rabid?" I guess. "You hardly ever hear about rabid ducks, but —"

"Do you want me to tell you this story or not?"

"I do."

"Where was I?"

"A duck and a guy. Riveting stuff, really."

"So, the duck keeps its grip on the guy's pant leg, won't let go. Finally the guy follows it over to a grate in the street. And he looks down and sees eight little ducklings looking up at him. So he calls the fire department and they come and rescue them. The mother duck waits until they're all safe and then off they waddle, back to the pond. Isn't that a great story?"

"Huh."

"Huh? That's all you have to say? It's a great story, Anna."

"I guess," I say.

"What do you mean, you guess?"

"Well, I was just thinking that it must have been against her instincts, really, to get that close to a human being, right?"

Isabel nods.

"She normally wouldn't have done that. But it was like something deeper was driving her, and so she took the risk."

"Yeah, to save her chicks."

"Well, that's how it turned out. But what if this tall human — enemy, really — had grabbed her by the neck and taken her home and cooked her for dinner. *Duck à l'orange*?"

Isabel leans back against the booth.

Sheilah comes with the hot chocolate. I say thank you and immediately spoon the whipped cream into my mouth. "Meanwhile, back at the sewer, the kids are wondering what's taking Mom so long. One chick says, 'I'll bet she's trying to flag down a human. You know, the kind she's always telling us to stay away from,' and another chick says, 'Don't be stupid.

Mom would never take a risk like that.' And a third chick says, 'Maybe she ran off with the cute mallard down the road.'"

And then I get it. As soon as the words "cute mallard" are out of my mouth, I get it. Isabel isn't telling me this stupid duck story because she wants to share a current-events moment. This is a good mother story.

"Oh," I say stupidly.

"So what do you think? My mom was trying to save my life or she ran off with the cute mallard?"

I don't say anything.

Isabel finishes her hot chocolate. "My bet is on the cute mallard."

"Isabel," I say. "I didn't mean —"

She holds up her hand like a crossing guard. "Please, no pity, okay? I'll puke, really. I've had two cheeseburgers, a large order of onion rings and three refilled ginger ales, so please. I couldn't stomach it."

"Maybe she just had to go."

"Are you saying she had no choice? Is that what you're saying?"

I shake my head. "No, I'm not. I guess we always have choices and I'm not saying she did the right thing, Isabel. I'm just saying … it's just … people always believe their own reasons, you know?"

Isabel digs around in her wallet for money, which she places on top of the bill. She gathers up her backpack and puts it on her lap, wrapping her arms around it.

"My ride's here." She nudges her head in the direction of the terminal. Sure enough, a small ferry is entering into the slip. "I'm going to Mayne Island."

"To see your mother?"

"Uh-huh. Mother Duck."

"Uh, about that, Isabel."

"Yeah, yeah. The fake e-mail. Your friends seriously need to work on their mail fraud schemes. Totally bogus."

"You knew? Then why are you going?"

"I was planning to go all along. I just thought I'd wait until camp was over. But it seemed pretty clear that ... well, my time was up. Don't worry about it."

"But you can't just leave."

She gives me a funny look. "I totally can."

I follow Isabel out the door, and Karim joins us.

"Hey," he says. "Vehicle is this way."

"Sorry, I have other plans." Isabel walks to the edge of the highway.

Karim looks confused. "Listen, you guys, as ridiculous as this sounds, I'm in charge here."

Isabel stops walking. "I don't want to get you in trouble, Karim, but I'm not going back. I ... can't." There is something in her voice that is immovable.

"Well," he finally says, "I have to get back. You be careful, okay? Seriously, Is, take care of yourself."

"I will." She walks across the highway after giving me the barest of waves. All I can think is that she looks like a brightly feathered duckling with a backpack. Where are the words when you need them? What can I say that will make her turn around and come back with us?

Isabel's crazy feather cap disappears into the ticket kiosk. She's about to board the ship that isn't invisible at all.

"Karim, I'm sorry."

He shrugs. "Let's get going."

But I don't move. "I'm going with her."

Karim groans. "Anna, you can't. I'm not allowed to lose two campers in one day."

"CITs," I correct. "I have to."

And then I run up to the edge of the highway.

"Anna," he shouts after me. "Truck!"

I stop just in time for a semi to speed by. I wave sheepishly to Karim, who is holding his face in his hands. "I totally saw it."

After I've purchased my ticket and a couple of chocolate bars from the vending machine, I board the ferry. I find Isabel outside on the deck. Déjà vu all over again. I hand her one of the bars. She looks surprised to see me.

"You're going to miss your race."

"Yeah, yeah."

"Everybody's going to hate you."

I peel the wrapper off of the bar and take a bite. "I always wondered what it would feel like to be on that list." It's a nice line, a brave line. I wish I believed it.

A ferry ride and a bus ride later, we stand at the top of a street lined with summer cottages. The rain has stopped; shrubs, trees and flowers glisten in the pale sunshine.

Isabel checks a crumpled piece of paper. She points to a small bungalow. "That's it, I think."

"Okay."

"I need to go by myself."

"Okay."

"I don't know how long I'll be."

"Okay."

"Stop saying okay."

"Okay."

She smiles, but her chin is trembling. "You shouldn't have come, Anna. You're missing the race. I — I don't know how long this will take."

"I'll wait."

"Seriously. You should just go back."

"I said I'll wait."

But Isabel doesn't move.

"You're scared," I say.

"I'm afraid. There's a difference."

"Not really. You just have to get your feet wet, remember?"

"Yeah, yeah."

"So float then."

She remains rooted. So much for words of inspiration. I cup my hands around my mouth and yell, "Hello! Anybody home?" A couple starlings fly out of the tree at the sudden blast of my voice.

Isabel glares at me, and then a woman appears from behind the house carrying a basket of flowers. She's wearing a pair of overalls and a baseball cap. She looks exactly like Isabel, except her hair is long and sandy colored.

"She's pretty," I say.

"Yeah." Isabel's voice is barely a whisper.

Then the woman sees Isabel, and she almost drops the basket. She smiles. I let out a sigh of relief and give Isabel a discreet little shove. "It's okay," I say.

Isabel shuffles slowly to where her mom is waiting. When she gets there, they stand with the gate between them. I can't hear the words. Then her mom reaches over and unlatches the gate. Isabel steps inside the yard and they hug for a long time. Mrs. Isabel looks at me over her daughter's shoulder and waves for me to come closer.

I just wave back. "I'll wait over there," I call, pointing to the beach.

They go inside the tiny house.

The tide is out and the view from here is pretty much the same as the view at camp. The clouds have rolled back, revealing patches of periwinkle sky.

I look at my watch. The race will be starting soon. My stomach flips over. Everyone will be waiting for me. I'm letting everyone down. I'm a deserter. I'll probably be shot at dawn. There will be blood.

But then I look over to the bungalow and my thoughts slow down. I should be panicky and anxious, but it feels like a blanket of calm has been spread over top of me, and it's warm. I'm not sure where it's come from, but I snuggle against it. I lean back against a log, and soon the only thing that I'm thinking about is the caressing touch of the wind.

I must have fallen asleep because Isabel is standing above me, looking very tall. "Let's go," she says.

I follow her up the street to the bus stop. I'm deadly curious, but we wait for the bus in silence. Then we sit on the bus in silence. Finally I can't stand it anymore. "So?"

"So, there's a ferry back to Kairos in an hour. I'm catching the one to the mainland."

The bus hits a pothole and we lurch forward.

"She's not coming back," Isabel says, looking straight ahead into the grimy headrest of the seat in front of us.

"Did you think she might?"

"Yep. That's what I thought." She twists her body suddenly. "That's actually what I thought! How stupid am I, Anna? Really. Tell me. Give me a new word. I need a new word for stupid. Idiotic? Thickheaded? Obtuse? Insane?"

"What did she say?"

"She's happy. That's what she said. She gave me a granola cookie and a glass of milk and told me she was happy." Her eyes are cloudy with tears. "A fucking glass of milk."

"That stinks, Isabel."

She keeps her face pasted against the window. From here, her hair doesn't look quite so vibrant. Her roots are showing and some of the colors are fading. I can see that her natural color is sandy blonde. And for some reason this makes me sad. She could really use the color right now.

"It's the truth," she says. "She's happy here. Without me. Without us." She shakes the sad hair. "I'm so stupid."

"Stop saying that."

"It's true. I just have to give up."

The bus lurches forward through a few more potholes and around sharp corners. It's practically empty and the driver is whistling. Finally I tug at Isabel's shirt. She doesn't respond at first, but then her head moves, just a little.

"You can't give up on her, Isabel."

"Why not? She's given up on me."

"But it's ... just not what you do."

Now she turns so that I can see her completely, and her face is wet with tears. Her eyes are so wide and full that it hurts to look at her.

"She shouldn't have left," I say. "Mothers shouldn't leave — that's the truth. But you don't give up on people, Isabel. You don't even believe in happy endings, and you still don't give up. You're so ... brave. You're so ... not-stupid."

Then we're both crying and I fumble in my pocket for tissues, which I don't have, of course. I find an old napkin and hand it to her. She takes it and blows her nose.

"That's your word for stupid? Not-stupid?"

"Yes."

"Anna?"

"Uh-huh."

"I don't think I could have gone in if I was alone."

Chapter Twenty-Three
Studies Say: Truth and Nuts Cause Indigestion

I buy two tickets for Kairos, but when I try to give one to Isabel, she shakes her head.

"I can't go back there."

"I'm not facing the music alone. No way."

Isabel considers this. Finally she says, "You may not have noticed, but I'm not exactly an asset to you."

The ferry horn blasts, and we're still on the wrong side of the gangplank.

"Nobody wants me there."

I give her a shove with my shoulder. "I want you there."

Surprisingly, she doesn't resist.

On the way back, I tell Isabel the whole Omnipotent Carrie/Cindy story. Right from the beginning to the bitter end — stink gesture and all.

"I didn't have to sign that petition," I say. "But I did. I was afraid they would do the same thing to me and I'd be a loser, a non-person, too."

Isabel doesn't respond. I would have tried to make me feel better. She doesn't. Finally, she says, "Poor Cindy."

"Yeah," I agree, kind of proud of myself for admitting to the whole thing. Not that it was my fault, but still. I could be big.

"She didn't even *do* anything."

"Uh-huh."

"She just wandered into the room, unsuspecting, talks about her cow and there she is — doomed."

"Well ..."

"Well what?" Isabel snaps.

"Well ... nothing, I guess."

"Well nothing? She walks into the room just trying to make friends, just trying to fit in, and boom — her life is ruined. Well nothing?" Isabel's voice is pretty loud; two grandmas, a kid and a man who was sleeping have turned to look at us.

"Are we still talking about Cindy?" I ask quietly, because she looks pretty mad.

"Yes," she erupts, and now the little kid has taken out his sandwich to eat it while he watches the show. "No," she says, only slightly less loudly. "Sometimes somebody has to do something."

Suddenly I can see why the girl doesn't float — she goes all the way to the bottom. "I guess we were scared to do anything. I was."

She says nothing, just turns and looks out the window.

The little kid is still staring, and he's starting to get on my last nerve. I make a face at him, but he doesn't budge. His mother glares at me. I ignore them both. "Sometimes people just suck, Isabel."

When the ferry docks at Kairos, I give the camp a quick call to let them know we'll catch the next bus and be there within the hour. There's no emotion in Old Betty's voice, but when she says that Big Jack will meet us at the gate, I detect a note of satisfaction. I've always suspected that a camper-in-trouble is probably the high point of her camp experience.

The bus drops us off at the gate and, sure enough, there he is, Scowling Big Jack.

We follow him into his office without a word.

He points us to a couple of chairs and then sits behind his desk. He tells us that we've missed the races, that our cabin has lost major points to Cabin Nine because of lack of team cohesiveness. He was moments away from calling the police to report us missing. We had put the camp through hell, and what did we have to say for ourselves?

"It's my fault," Isabel says.

"No, it's not," I falter a little under the weight of Big Jack's glower, but I plow ahead. Mr. Hong is whispering his plea for truth (*it shall set you free*), but I'm not sure that's quite enough. This might require more drastic measures. Maybe even a little finesse. Possibly embellishment.

"Remember the day at the beginning of camp when I was outside cleaning bottles?"

Big Jack's big head nods up and down. Once, slowly.

"You said that sometimes a person just has to figure out how to do things a different way?"

I have discovered that sometimes, with parents for instance, it really helps your case if you work their sayings into the conversation. "Remember? I was trying to figure out how to get the straw out of the bottle? And that's when you —"

"This isn't really the same thing, though, is it, Anna?"

"No, I guess not." My brain scurries ahead to look for something new. "Don't you think ... doesn't it seem sometimes that life is like a plane?" Out of the corner of my eye, I think I see Isabel smile. She can't be serious. "And we're all pilots, you know, of our own planes. When things are going smoothly then we're, like, on autopilot, but sometimes things get a little, well, turbulent and then we have to land the plane on our own."

Big Jack sits there like Big Jack Mountain.

"What about the air-traffic controller?" Isabel asks out of the side of her mouth.

I don't even look at her. "Well, sure. Sometimes the guy is helpful, but maybe he's drunk?" I glare at her quickly and then turn back to Big Jack. "Or maybe there's this big fog so you just put your hands on the controls and look for the runway lights and do your best. On your own."

There is utter silence, and it's starting to feel really hot in here.

"Of course," I continue. "You hope the lights are the runway, I guess, and not a mall. Or maybe —"

Isabel groans. "What Anna is trying to say, and what I want to say, is that we're really sorry. I was wrong to leave without telling anyone. Anna convinced Karim to come and get me because she wanted to help me. And she did. But I'm sorry that you were worried about us."

Big Jack smiles. "Thank you."

And then there's the simple approach.

We lug the buckets and disinfectants to the boys' bathroom. "It's going to be even more disgusting than the last time."

"Yeah. I can't believe your plane story didn't win him over."

"It was an analogy, not a story."

"Oh. Excuse me," she says. "My favorite was the part about hoping that you don't fly into a mall."

In the dank depths of the boys' bathroom Isabel is still laughing.

By the time we've finished scouring the filthy walls (and lost what's left of our innocence), I can tell from the noise that the final bonfire and wienie roast is taking place, but I've lost my appetite and am more than a little nervous about running into Cabin Seven.

We meet Shell on the path. She races up and gives Isabel a hug. Then she pushes her away to look at her, like she might have changed in the six hours she's been gone.

"Are you okay? What happened? You really scared us, you know."

Between the two of us we explain and apologize until Shell holds up her hand. She's heard enough. "As long as you're okay, I don't care. Jennifer's the one who's pissed off. Have you considered the Witness Protection Program?"

We laugh weakly.

"Well, if you think that's funny, you should have seen her face when Cabin Nine received commendation for Best Team Cabin."

"Where is everybody?"

"The Talent Show just started. I'll be right there. You guys go ahead."

"Ugh, I have to shower first," says Isabel. "Anna?"

"I'm going to go find Zoe. I need to talk to her."

"Do you want me to come with you?"

I hesitate. "I better go alone."

Shell and Isabel continue to the cabin. I'm tempted to join them, but I need to talk to Zoe. Maybe I'll puke first. I can't believe I'm so nervous! This is nuts. Totally nuts. Macadamia. Brazil. Almond.

I find myself straining to think of every single nut

I've ever encountered in my life in order to calm myself as I walk the path to the firepit where the talent show is taking place. Hazel. Cashew. Peanut! How could I forget the lowly peanut? The most common nut of all, and what a nut it is. Shelled or unshelled, salted or unsalted, buttered or candied. Sometimes toffee and chocolate is involved. Honestly, the versatility of the peanut is positively inspiring.

And then I have to stop walking because I really am feeling nauseous. Probably the damn nuts.

When I get to the firepit, my cabinmates are sitting together at the far end. Beverley's cabin is up on the stage, and I don't want to interrupt the delicate production of the Spit Skit.

In all the years I've seen it performed, it's been a boy who ends up drinking the foul contents of the toothpaste cup. But this year, Beverley stands at the end of the line. At first I think it must be a mistake. Maybe she's just biding her time, waiting for her chance to spring *King Lear* on everyone when they least expect it.

But after everyone has gargled and spit into the cup, she makes her way to the center of the stage, grabs the cup and bolts down the wretched concoction.

The crowd groans loudly at first, but then there are cheers of admiration (and some gagging). Beverley grins from ear to ear and wipes her mouth. Then she rubs her stomach and says loudly, "Good to the last drop."

Well, this is a new line, and I clap for her improvisation. She sees me and I raise my arms and clap even harder. Then I give her the thumbs up, which she returns with a broad, goofy smile. She is so proud of herself. "Good for you," I mouth. Her little buddies are patting her on the back. Even some of the boys seem impressed. I watch her leave the stage, surrounded by her new admirers. I guess everybody's scary thing is a little different. Hers was to not get her own way, probably for the first time.

Well, it was time for my scary thing. I'd run out of nuts, so to speak. As I head over to Zoe, I rehearse what I will say. It goes something like this. "Er, um, well, Zoe." That's about all I have when I sneak up behind her and tap her on the shoulder. She jumps when she sees me.

"Can I talk to you?" I whisper.

We walk over to the Honesty Tree, which is appropriate, I guess. I can feel Jennifer's glare on my back the whole way.

"Where did you go? You missed everything. Everybody is really upset."

"I had to find Isabel."

"That took all afternoon?"

"No."

"So, what then? Where did you go?"

"Look, I just wanted to tell you that I'm sorry I missed the race and everything."

"That's it? You're not going to tell me what happened?"

The truth. The truth. I need the truth. See, now this is tricky. Can I tell Zoe what she wants to hear?

(And what is that anyway?) Do I tell her what happened with Isabel without breaking a confidence? In fact, I'm not so sure I really get truth, when it comes right down to it. It's too huge. Truth should come in a variety pack: individual servings for everyday use.

"Everybody was really disappointed. We were counting on you." She looks like she wants to say something else — the words coming out of her mouth are not the words sitting behind her eyes.

"Really, Zoe? Did you want me to race?" I blurt out.

"What's that supposed to mean?'

"Listen, I'm sorry I wasn't here, and I'm sorry I let everyone down, but, honestly, did you even think I had a chance at winning the race?"

"That wasn't the point and you know it. By not showing up, you made sure that Cabin Seven wouldn't win the Best Cabin award. And that looks bad for all of us."

"You've never ever cared about winning the team award, Zoe."

Okay. Sometimes truth just lands at your feet in a lump, like a big, dead bird falling out of the sky. No warning.

"Nice, Anna."

And then Jennifer is standing beside Zoe. She doesn't say a word to me, barely even looks at me. She just gives Zoe a consoling smile and says, "You don't need this loser." Then she takes her by the arm and leads her back to the Talent Show.

I stand there under the branches of the Honesty Tree. More dead birds of truth fall down all around me. Loser? Had I always been the loser here? Was that why Zoe was my friend, to make sure someone else was always second best? So that she would always be first?

There had to be losers so other people could feel like winners. People like Isabel, people like Cindy S, people like me. We made other people feel like they were better. This is truth?

Then, truth sucks, too.

Chapter Twenty-Four
Missing "i" in Sprit: Found

The atmosphere the next morning is what I imagine a morgue would be like: chilly and dank with the lingering awareness of endings. We pack up our stuff and haul it outside to be picked up by the vans that will take us to the ferry terminal. As each load is removed, the cabin returns slowly to its former state. It's like we were never here, except for a few more initials carved in the bedposts. But I know it's changed for me. Because I've changed. And Zoe and I have changed.

There are still a couple of hours before we leave. Everyone is wandering around, saying good-bye, signing scraps of paper, handing out e-mail addresses and phone numbers, making promises of eternal devotion and friendship. (Ha.) When I walk past the Honesty Tree, I see Karim and Isabel. They call me over.

"Hey, how did it go with Zoe last night? You went to bed so early, I didn't get a chance to talk to you," Isabel says.

"It, uh, didn't go real well."

"I'm sorry."

"Yeah, well, what'cha gonna do?"

"She'll come around," says Karim.

I know they're trying to reach me, but I've mostly gone home already. I don't trust myself to speak.

Jennifer and Zoe are over at the trampoline with Jake, Owen, Charmaine, Benita and the others. They're all there and they're all laughing, and I don't know any of them any better than I did before the summer.

Zoe doesn't look happy, though. Or maybe it's just wishful thinking on my part. She's made it onto Jennifer's Sun — she should be happy.

Then my own sunshine is blocked and I see Arlene, Behemoth of the Deep, standing in front of me.

"Missed you yesterday," she says.

"Yeah. Congratulations on the race." She had won, of course.

She squats down in front of me. "Well, between you and me" — she turns to Karim and Isabel, who are both pretending not to listen — "and you guys. It wasn't much of a challenge without you."

"Yeah, well, what'cha gonna do?" This is my new saying, I think. It will serve me well for the rest of my life.

"You could race me."

"Uh, well, what?"

"I heard you had a way with words."

"That is an awesome idea!" Isabel says.

"Totally," adds Karim, and we all stare at him. "Just trying to fit in." He shrugs. "C'mon ... there's time before we leave."

"Well, have fun, kids," I say.

"C'mon, Anna Banana. This is your moment. I can feel it in the marrow of my bones," says Isabel.

"Your marrow is mistaken."

"My marrow is never mistaken."

"I don't even have a bathing suit on."

"Oh, well, can't swim without a bathing suit," says Karim.

"We're both wearing shorts. We'll be equally dis-advantaged," says Arlene.

I cast a look down her bronzed, muscled torso. "Yeah, right."

"I'll meet you at the wharf," she says, as if she's tiring of this conversation. "Don't keep me waiting." And then she strides away. Seriously, she strides.

"Well, I hope she has a nice time," I mutter, my bum still firmly affixed to the ground.

"I'll go wait with her," says Isabel. "Take your time. Psychological warfare. Good job, Anna." She gives me a big wink and then she, too, is off.

"They're both delusional."

"You're just having a few pre-race jitters," Karim says. "Perfectly normal."

"I'm not jittering. There are no jitters here. I am

jitter-free. I'm just waiting for the van and not getting into trouble."

"I've seen both of you swim. You can compete with her."

"Yeah, well, it's not happening."

"Listen to me, you freaking idiot. When you don't think too much, the way you swim is natural. It's like you were born to it. All you have to do is show up."

"You freaking idiot?"

"Anna, this is your scary thing."

"Um, no. I did two scary things yesterday. I went after Isabel, and I found out a really gross, horrible truth about my best friend and me. That's my scary quota for the year."

"What gross, horrible truth did you find out?"

"That she isn't ... that we aren't what I thought we were."

"So then, be something else."

I pick a daisy and start dismembering it. I pluck the petals off one by one. I get down to the last three petals when I figure out what I'm whispering on the other side of my thoughts. *Race. Don't Race.* I pull the last petal free. *Race.* Stupid daisy.

"Why should I do this, Karim? Really."

His hand reaches up to touch his shoulder and at first I think it's that involuntary reflex, that invisible thing. But he leans forward and pulls his T-shirt up to reveal the scar. He shrugs and slips the shirt over it again. "Because you can."

"Shit."

"I know," he smiles. "Dirty trick. But, Anna, a race is just about the race — it's not personal. You do it because you can."

I get up and wipe the grass off my bum. I don't look at him, but I know he's following me as I head down to the wharf.

The shore pulses with people. We attract a few curious stares as Arlene and I make our way down to the end of the wharf, and then I hear Marcus yell, "Hey, what's going on?"

I give Isabel a quick look. "Great. Now if we could just alert the media, that would be perfect."

"I'm on it," she says, then she gives me a quick hug. "Break a leg."

"No," I moan. "You don't say that for swimming."

"Oh ... grow a fin?"

My fingers are balled up into fists at my side and the muscles in my legs feel bound together. As I move to the edge of the wharf — the starting line — I try to remember even one thing that I've been taught about swimming, but it's as though someone has come along and emptied my brain. Don't think too much. *A race is just about the race.* Okay, okay.

Arlene stands beside me with her broad shoulders, strong upper body, narrow hips and powerful legs. Her hair is up in a ponytail, and I realize that she has absolutely zero body hair. This is not even natural. I don't want to look at her, but it's like looking at an accident. I can't help myself.

Then she turns to me and I can see the intense concentration in her eyes. "Good luck," I say gruffly.

Her head tilts. She surprises me by smiling. "Same," she says. "Don't you love this?"

Ba-doyng. That's the sound a new thought makes when it vibrates inside your empty head. Except it's not exactly new. I've known this all my life. It's so stupid. It's so simple. How could I have forgotten this?

I love swimming.

Karim's whistle comes through a haze. There is a flurry of motion and then I'm the only one standing on the dock. A disturbance below indicates that Arlene has dived into the water.

"Go." I hear, from somewhere around me, or inside me. My feet tip forward, setting everything else into motion.

As my arms submerge in front of me, the noise of cheering fades into a distant roar. The only thing I hear besides the blood pumping in my ears is "I love this."

Then something else comes as a whisper. Two words.

My right arm pulls water back to me. *Just.* My left side matches the stroke with equal power. *Be.* My right arm pulls again and then I breathe. My lungs take in air greedily and then I do it all over again, and it feels right. I stretch as far as I can, pull back as hard as I can. I kick.

There are no questions, no doubts. Not even a wondering, just a knowing. I'm part of the water, the sky, the wind, the churning of the wake produced by

Arlene, who is part of this one thing as well — the race. It's so simple, this knowing. It's everything. It's enough to be here. I'm enough. And so I swim. And I swim. And I swim.

I don't even realize that I've made the turn at the halfway-point buoy until there is the unmistakable feeling of sand and pebbles beneath my feet. I feel the thin rope in my hand and it's all over.

This is new to me, this scratchy feeling of finishing line twine in my fingers. I open my eyes and look behind me. Arlene's form is perfect. She is still swimming. And then she's standing as well.

We look at each other. She seems surprised. She digs both hands into the water and splashes me full in the face. I have to rub my eyes for a second because it's salt water, but when I can see again, she's grinning and shaking her head.

"Now *that* was a race," she says.

All I can do is stand there and soak it in. Sorry about the pun but, honestly, I can't even really think yet. It's all so new, this winning. It's weird, it's different. And I realize that the other thing I felt — that everything feeling, that oneness of the race — is slipping away. This being first is a separation.

And then the others are splashing around me: Charmaine, Benita, Gin and Mags congratulate me. And then they're splashing each other, and Jake and Owen join in. It becomes a free-for-all. Jennifer isn't among the group — I guess she doesn't do free-for-alls. Neither is Zoe.

Isabel picks her way through the water, gingerly.

"Good race, Anna," she says.

"Well, look at you, all standing in the ocean and everything."

"Yeah, yeah." She looks around as though she's expecting something vile to wrap its slimy self around her. "I'll be back on dry land if you need me." She starts back, but then she turns. "Zoe was cheering for you."

"Really?" I try to see if I can spot Zoe on the shore, but she's nowhere. I walk back with Isabel.

"She might have left with the first van," Isabel says. "She was standing beside me during the race, and then she was gone. I'm sorry."

"It doesn't matter."

I dry myself off with a towel and we sit under the old Honesty Tree to wait for the next van. Suddenly, Marcus plummets down from the branches above. It's a good fall: he doesn't seem to have sustained any injuries.

"How long have you been waiting to do that?" I ask.

He picks himself up. "A while." He looks right past me to Isabel. "Hey, Is."

"Hey, Marcus. Nice form."

He scoots between us and sits down on the grass. Apparently I've become invisible. I get up. "I'm just going to see if I can ..." I start to explain, but no one is listening. They're discussing the art of tree-falling. "I'll be back," I add, just in case.

Zoe is standing on the other side of the tree. She has a plastic bag wrapped around her cast. "I was going to come into the water to see you ... to say ... but you were gone."

"To say what?"

She takes a breath. "You swam extravagantly."

"Wow. Nice word."

"I wanted a good one."

"Thanks," I say, and then the air is awkward between us.

"I'm sorry," she says.

"You don't have to be," I say quickly. "I don't want you to be sorry."

"Why?" Suddenly she's indignant. "I can be sorry, you know."

"I just don't want you to *have* to be ... sorry. I just —"

"Oh, shut up. I'm sorry and that's it. I didn't know you could swim like that!"

"Neither did I."

"Shut up," she says again. "Yes, you did. You were amazing and I didn't know. Maybe I didn't want to know." She shrugs. "I just have to win, you know?"

"You're really saying 'you know' a lot."

"Shut up."

"And 'shut up.' That was the third time, I think."

"I have to win because that's what I do. But I don't *have* to win." Her eyes fill up with tears and I know they're the real thing. And not one bit invisible.

They're falling down her cheeks. "You just had a BTBD, and I got to see it!"

"You were with me in *sprit*," I say. And then I'm crying and we hug. "I'm sorry, too," I say. She nods. "But Isabel is my friend, okay?"

She nods. "I know."

"And we gotta stop calling people *extras*."

She nods again, still sniffling. "That's kind of what I've been thinking. It sorta sucks."

"It sorta does," I agree. "But who's the cutest girl in a cast?"

"I am!" And then we're giggling, which is the best thing to do under almost any circumstances.

Suddenly the van honks, and I realize that I can't leave. "Make them wait for me, okay?" I say to Zoe.

"Where are you going?"

"To say good-bye to ... someone."

Zoe squints her eyes. "Do you have something you need to tell me?"

"Later," I yell over my shoulder. "Don't let them leave without me!"

"I'll throw myself into the middle of the road if I have to," she yells back.

I smile about this all the way to the pool because I know it's true.

Karim is pulling the tarp over the water. I pick up a corner and help him pull it to the end. It rolls up and over the sparkling blue water like we're putting it to bed and tucking it in.

"See ya," I say to the water, as it disappears from view.

Karim smiles in his familiar, condescending way. He sits down on one of the bleachers, leans back in his familiar, cool way. I perch on the edge.

"It was a pretty race," he says.

"You left."

"You were surrounded. But it was pretty."

I can see that there was a cost for him, watching the race, watching me swim. "You're a good coach."

"Thanks."

"I mean it. When I was on the wharf I was afraid to dive in and your voice was there. It helped."

"You dove in all by yourself."

"Not nearly. You're a good coach."

"It's not the same."

"No." I want to say more, convince him, but I don't. I sit there. But it's hard, and I actually have to bite my lip.

"Oh, just say it."

"Say what?"

"Whatever you're trying so hard not to say."

"I was fine not saying anything. I'm actually quite capable of not talking every minute of every hour of every ..."

"What?"

I sigh. "Just that maybe it's a different ending? Coaching. Maybe it's time to be something else. A very bossy person once said that to me."

The horn from the van bellows three long blasts. Three deafening, unexpected blasts. It shouldn't come as a big surprise — this is what departing vans do.

"I better go," I say, but I don't move. I lean back on the bleachers and our shoulders are almost touching. Almost.

"So, do you think you'll come back next year?" he asks.

"Are you going to be here?"

"Maybe."

I wait a couple of seconds. "Then probably not."

He actually laughs at this, shows his white teeth in a completely non-sarcastic way, and I think this may be my favorite accomplishment of a very weird summer. I get up and walk over to the exit in a dignified fashion, although my bum might still be a little wet.

"Hey, Lipgloss."

"What?"

"You know, right?"

"Know what?"

"I don't not like you."

Later, wedged between Zoe and Isabel on the ferry, I tell them everything. "Do you think I should have said something after he said he didn't not like me?"

Isabel snorts. "Like ask for clarification?"

"Oh, no," Zoe says reassuringly. "It's good to play it cool. Guys love that."

"Really?" I say.

Isabel and Zoe look at each other and then crack up.

"You guys are quite a team," I say.

And I have to laugh, too. The sound of us travels out across the mauve water, over the emerald trees, and back in waves to Kairos.

Mr. Hong will want the facts (*just the facts, ma'am*) about what I did this summer. This is what I will say ...

I learned that life is complicated and simple.

I think there are facts, and there is truth. Sometimes they're connected, and sometimes they aren't.

I think Karim is cute, and I think that Zoe is changing. So am I.

I think that nobody knows who they are all at once — maybe it would be too much. I think we get glimpses, but we never know for sure how we're going to turn out. And guess what, Mr. Hong? Maybe there is such a thing as varnished truth, coat after coat after coat, but the color always shows through.

Maybe that's just the way life is: lots of crazy, shimmering colors you never imagined, in corners you never looked into before.

I like to think of it as the Isabel Factor.

Also by Gayle Friesen

Janey's Girl

After this summer, nothing would ever be the same. Fourteen-year-old Claire's trip across the country with her mother unlocks the key to many questions Claire has about her past — including the identity of her father.

"In this well-written first novel, Friesen tells an involving story. The author is particularly adept at revealing the many emotions of the various characters." — *School Library Journal*

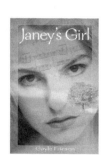

"A stunning debut. The main characters are real — interesting and imperfect." — *Quill & Quire*

• Red Maple Award
• Violet Downey Book Award
• Junior Library Guild Selection
• The New York Public Library Books for the Teen Age List

Men of Stone

Living in a house full of women isn't helping fifteen-year-old Ben make sense of his life. Then Great-Aunt Frieda comes to visit and Ben learns about her former life in Russia. He's amazed at how she dealt with the Men of Stone — Stalin's agents who terrorized her community and family. As Frieda tells her powerful story, Ben begins to gain perspective on his own life.

"A captivating tale … engaging enough to interest even reluctant readers." — *School Library Journal*

"Very well-written; Ben is a fully realized, funny and charming character." — *Kirkus Reviews*

• Society of School Librarians International Honor Book
• Children's Literature Annual Top Choices List
• Parent's Guide to Children's Media Award

Losing Forever

For Jes, normal life is slipping away. Her mother is totally preoccupied with getting married again and Jes's best girlfriend has fallen for a complete jerk. To make matters worse, Jes also has to deal with Angela, her soon-to-be stepsister, who has come to stay. A half-crazed mother, a lovesick friend, a perfectly evil stepsister — could things for Jes get any worse?

Addressing relevant themes such as coping with change, dealing with divorce and falling in love, *Losing Forever* is a novel that speaks to young adults in an unsentimental voice.

"Friesen convincingly and respectfully handles Jes's anxiety as she negotiates these not-so-everyday trials." — *Horn Book Guide*

"Particularly well-crafted." — *Booklist*

- Red Maple Award
- CLA Young Adult Book of the Year Award
- The New York Public Library Books for the Teen Age List
- Society of School Librarians International Honor Book